W9-AOP-933

KENDRICK

Other books by A. H. Holt:

Silver Creek

KENDRICK

·

A.H. Holt

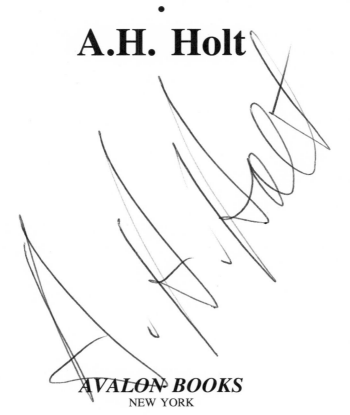

AVALON BOOKS
NEW YORK

© Copyright 2004 by A.H. Holt
Library of Congress Catalog Card Number: 2003097362
ISBN 0-8034-9650-8
All rights reserved.
All the characters in this book are fictitious,
and any resemblance to actual persons,
living or dead, is purely coincidental.
Published by Thomas Bouregy & Co., Inc.
160 Madison Avenue, New York, NY 10016

PRINTED IN THE UNITED STATES OF AMERICA
ON ACID-FREE PAPER
BY HADDON CRAFTSMEN, BLOOMSBURG, PENNSYLVANIA

To my father,
Richardson Wallace Haw, III,
who taught me to love books

Chapter One

The cup sailed over my head and crashed against the wall. Coffee and pieces of china flew over half the kitchen floor. I could feel drops of hot coffee hitting the back of my left shoulder.

Me and Millie started arguing while I was trying to eat my breakfast. I got so angry with her I went and said something really stupid. Something I should never even think, much less actually come right out and say to somebody. When I said it, she didn't even answer me. I happened to look up in time to catch a glimpse of her arm moving. That cup would have caught me right alongside my head if I hadn't ducked.

I couldn't believe she did it. I stood up to stare at Millie in astonishment. She slapped one hand over her mouth and stared right back at me. I think she was every bit as surprised I was. After a second or two of staring her eyes began to fill up with tears. She put both hands up to her face and dashed out of the room. I could hear her sobbing out loud as she ran up the steps and down the hall to her room.

First thing I thought of was to clean up the mess. There was coffee and pieces of that cup everywhere. On second thought, it come to me that the best thing I could do for Millie was to grab my hat and coat and get myself out of the house for a few hours.

Shutting the door carefully so not to let it slam, I stepped out on the porch. I needed to go to Belden anyway—been putting it off for days. The trip would take me most of the day. That ought to give Millie time enough to calm herself down.

The sun was just edging itself up over top of the mountains when I led my pony out beside the corral and threw my saddle up on his back. All the lights were out in the bunkhouse. The only sign of activity I could see was in the cook shack where Billy Dunn would be cleaning up after cooking breakfast for the crew. The riders would all be out on the range by now.

I poked my knee into Rollo's fat belly and yanked the cinch strap tight before he could get his breath good. That fool pony's got a slick trick of blowing his belly up so's he can get the saddle loose. He tossed his head around when he knew I'd caught him in his meanness and jangled his bit at me. The devious little skunk. He knows every dirty trick a horse can think of and is always trying to toss me in the dirt. Anybody would think he was part mule.

After trying my saddlebags and canteen securely behind the saddle I mounted, pulling hard on the reins at the same time. You couldn't let Rollo get his fool head down. He danced around kind of sideways for a few steps and then pretended to give in. I held him tight though. He'd caught me sleeping before and thrown me on my butt. I wasn't about to give the blasted jughead another chance to put me on the ground.

It galls me to have to take a day away from the ranch, but I've got some important business in town. I've been laying off to take a day and go to Belden to get some cash money to pay the regular hands. It's about time for me to hire six or seven extra riders to help us out with spring roundup too. I always put the trip off as long as I can. The doggoned town is just far enough away from the ranch to be aggravating. It takes long enough to get there as it is. I don't have time to be fooling around with this maverick pony.

Me and my sister—Millie that is—have been running the ranch together for two years now. Ever since our Dad died. She's the foreman in the house and barns and I run the show with the cattle and horses mostly, then we work on the infernal bookkeeping together.

We don't fight over things often, but Millie's got her way of thinking and I've got mine. That's the way most folks are, I reckon. But we both got up on the wrong side of our beds this morning.

That woman's got her a wild notion lately that she wants us to buy some highfalutin kind of bull to improve our herd. She read about the thing in some newspaper or other. I think the critter's from Scotland or maybe it's another foreign place. I'm not sure. Well as it happens, I like the bulls we've got.

Besides, it appears to me that Millie's real problem is she knows we've got a bit of money laid by and she's itching to spend it on something or other. We started out just talking about buying that bull, but now we've been arguing over it for more than a week.

That woman's about as stubborn as this clabber-headed yahoo I'm trying to ride when she gets something stuck in her head. This morning, I got brave and said a nasty thing about women folks sticking their noses in men's business. Then Millie got so fretted over me making that crack that I'll be doggoned if she didn't haul off and throw that coffee cup at me. Maybe I deserved it. I don't know. But it looks like Millie and me are both gonna have to say "I'm sorry" more than once before we get over this fracas.

There's a lot of work to running a ranch the size of ours. To be fair, Millie's about as good a partner as a man could find. We've got a good foreman, too. Rich Thomas started working for us maybe four or five years before our Dad died. It would be hard to think of running the place without him now.

He was the first one to get to the house the morning Dad passed away. At first Dad looked like he was sleeping real peaceful like. The Doc told us later that it was a heart attack that killed him. He seemed to think Dad had died in his sleep and never knew what hit him.

Rich was a right smart help to us then. He still is. He could probably run the ranch a whole lot better and at a bigger profit if me and Millie would just keep our noses out of things.

As soon as Rollo calmed down a little bit I eased up on his reins enough so he could trot out between the barns. I took the dirt lane that connects to the road to town. By the time I cleared the ranch buildings that ornery sucker had decided to quit his foolishness. He commenced to jog along easy, eating up the miles.

I complain about Rollo a lot, but I actually enjoy riding him. Even being sore at Millie can't take anything away from that. He's a fine looking horse: compact and short-coupled with a slick-looking black hide. And he'll work, I tell you. He's probably the best cow horse I've ever seen. It's just a darn shame he has to act so ornery every single morning.

By the time I got off ranch property and started down the main road the sun was full up. It looked as if the day would build up to a real scorcher. We get desert weather here oftentimes, even this early in the spring. The sun tries to cook you in the daytime, and you have to wrap yourself up in a heavy quilt to keep from freezing at night. Soon I got so warm I took my jacket off and stuffed it down in one of my saddlebags. Then I settled down to get myself to Belden.

My head was still full of that crazy argument with Millie. As I kept thinking over what was said before we both blew up, it come to me that she had been acting a little different the last couple of weeks anyway. Millie's ten years younger than I am. She's always been "baby sister," to me, but she's no baby, especially when she loses her temper.

Come to think of it, Millie's gonna have her twenty-first birthday the fifth of next month. Maybe she's just generally upset because we've had the care of the ranch these last two years, and she's getting older and ain't had a chance to get out and kick up her heels none.

I don't know if that could be it or not. I don't rightly understand the way women folks think about things like that. I know she's been sort of moody lately, like she had something on her mind.

Rollo kind of sunfished as we passed by the big stone posts that sit on either side of the entrance to Major Cason's place. He does that every single time I ride him past here. It's hard to blame him. I can't help but shake my head when I see those crazy piles of stone sticking up. You'd think royalty lived there or something.

In a way I guess it does. The only woman I ever thought to marry does, anyway. Meg Cason was a pest following her brother and me around for years, but all of a sudden she was a grown up lady and I couldn't take my eyes off her. That was when the Major sent her off to Boston to go to school.

Meg stayed East for more than four long years. I was sort of courting Sue Lane, the banker's daughter, when Meg came home. The first time I went over to Cason's place and saw her again I knew I was just wasting my time with Sue. Meg was what I wanted. I guess she always was.

But when I went over there again the next week and asked her to go to a dance in town that Saturday night, Meg yelled at me that she didn't go to dances with men

who were promised to other girls. Before I could say a
word she turned around, marched out of the room, and
slammed the door.

Now Sue Lane's been married to some storekeeper from
Denver for more than two years. I heard somebody say she
had twin girls and was in a family way again. But from
that day to this if I ask for Meg, either the Major or his
son Jim tell me she's too busy to see me.

It's sort of puzzling to me. I've run into her out on the
range two different times lately. Each of those times she's
ridden alongside me for a few minutes and pointedly asked
me why I've been such a stranger. Now that's sort of a
puzzle too, because up until early last fall, I was making
myself a regular pest by going over there so often. At least
that's the way I had gotten to feeling about it. I wonder
sometimes if maybe it ain't Jim and Major Cason that don't
want me to see Meg.

All those things kept jumping around in my head all the
way to town. It made the trip seem like it would take forever. When I finally got to town, and made the turn past
the livery stable, I was out and out flabbergasted to see that
the street was jammed full of wagons, buggies, and people.

Everywhere I looked, all I could see was people and
more people. Most of the folks I saw were men, but here
and there I spotted women and some kids. They were sitting up on wagon seats, walking along the street, and going
in and out of the mercantile. People were crowding in the
saloon and every one of the stores and shops along the
street.

I'll tell you what. The sight plumb dumbfounded me. I
ain't never seen so many people in the same place anywhere. I certainly never dreamed I would see such a crowd
on the main street of Belden. Why, I'd bet a dollar there's
not that many people living in all of Custer County.

Pulling my hat down to shade my eyes, I stood up in
my stirrups so I could look over the multitude and try to

see anybody recognizable. It gave me an actual feeling of relief when I finally spotted Tom Dillard, our town sheriff. I could see his white head sticking up over the crowd. He was standing on the sidewalk in front of his office. His deputy, Ollie Foster, was standing right alongside him.

Them two stood there, leaning back against the front of the building, just watching the folks in the street. I figure they were as amazed at the sight as I was. That crowd of strangers milling around seemed like some sort of a show.

I walked Rollo around the wagons and buggies and through groups of people until I worked myself over to the hitch rail in front of the store porch. There was so many people it looked hopeless to try and get a horse across the street. I stepped down and made my way across to the other side on foot. When I got near enough so Tom could hear me over the crazy ruckus, I yelled.

"What the Sam Hill's happening around here, Tom? I've never seen so many people in all my life 'less it was up in Denver. Did the whole blasted world decide to come to visit?"

Tom Dillard always takes the time to screw his mouth up and spit tobacco sideways before he can say a word. I propped the toe of my left boot up on the edge of the board sidewalk and leaned my elbow on my knee to wait him out.

Tom finally got started talking and said, "How you doing today, Kendrick? Ain't this something? All them folks you see wandering around here is headed up to Shell Mountain to dig for gold. Some fancy dude come in town around the middle of last month claiming he had found some color up there. I don't know how the word spread so fast, but by now you'd think he'd found another Comstock Lode."

It was a big surprise to me to hear him say that. You can bank on that. I had a special interest in Shell Mountain. I stepped up on the boardwalk so me and the Sheriff could talk better. I needed to know more about this.

"Would it happen that I know this fella you're talking about?"

My head was going a mile a minute. *What in the world was going on here*, I was wondering. The more Tom Dillard talked the harder I had to work to keep a straight face. I didn't want to give myself away to the sheriff, but my belly felt all hollow-like and I was beginning to be some kinda worried.

Jim Cason, Meg's brother and my best friend, started himself a homestead up at the top of the valley, right there on Shell Mountain. He had been working on it over the last couple of years. His place sits over on the eastern-most side of the lake, and his claim covers almost the whole top of the mountain.

Sheriff Dillard hitched up his pants a time or two and shrugged, then he finally answered me. "I don't think so, Ken. Nobody around here knowed the man. Least ways, I ain't talked to nobody that'll own up to knowing him. I seen him out a my office window when he first rode in town. He was up on a fine looking roan gelding. He come down the street past my office to go to the assayer's place. Me and Ollie was sitting here passing the time of day, like we do most days, but I kind of like to pay attention to strangers when they come in town. I reckon he stayed in the assay office for about as long as I ever seen anybody stay there, 'ceptin maybe the assayer himself. He was down there for a particular long spell, anyway."

"Tom, what exactly do you mean by a long spell?" I asked, beginning to feel impatient and a little irritated with Tom's roundabout way of talking. I was wondering what in the world the man staying at the assay office a long time could have to do with anything.

"Well, I reckon he maybe stayed in there a good hour and a half. Or, I don't rightly know for sure, it mighta even been nearer to two hours." Dillard continued talking at his own pace, ignoring my show of impatience.

He turned to his deputy for confirmation, "Don't you reckon it was the best part of two hours that fella was down there, Ollie?"

After Ollie nodded his agreement to Tom's estimate of how long the man had stayed at the assay office, the Sheriff started up telling the story again, taking his time with it, as he usually did.

I knew there was no need for me to try to rush him any. Me and plenty of other people around this town have tried to do it, more times than once, but Tom just goes along talking at his own pace.

"When that fella finally come out of the assay office, I watched him walk down past here. He was leading that roan horse then. The next thing he did was to go over yonder to Judge Stern's place. The Judge told me later that the man come in his office to file a homestead claim on most of the whole top of Shell Mountain. I hear tell he's living up there now. He's got himself a mine office in a little cabin. Calls it the Blake Mining Company. I reckon he's making most of his money offa selling the right to mine gold to folks like these here pilgrims cluttering up our town."

"Have you been up there?" I asked.

"I took me a ride up there early last week. I didn't have no particular law reason to go up there, but I did it anyhow. I thought I'd just sort of check around some. A miner stopped by here one day and told Ollie here a long kinda mixed-up story about some of them miners going missing from the diggings."

"What did he mean by that?"

"He said some of the men that were working claims up there were going missing. I don't rightly know exactly what he did mean Ken, besides meaning exactly what he said. Well of course you know, it ain't rightly my lookout what goes on up there anyway. Any lawbreaking on the mountain would be for the county sheriff to be worrying about, not me. Shell Mountain's right close by here though, and the county seat is a pretty far piece away. Come to think of it, I ain't never yet seen that County Sheriff or even one of his deputies over in these here parts. Anyhow, I decided I would go on up there and poke around some. I figured those miners were more than like just going on home cause they weren't finding no gold, not really disappearing. But I was getting downright curious to have me a look at the place. That man's story about miners disappearing made me all the excuse I needed to stick my nose in a little. When I got up there that Blake was standing behind a counter in his office looking downright important. I asked him if he knew anything about men going missing and he got all puffed up and said it was all a lie that had been made up on purpose to try to cause him trouble. He allowed that the men that were supposed to be gone missing had only just given up looking for gold and left the diggings, or either they had found what they come for and gone on back home."

"Where's this man's office?" I asked.

"It's in a snug little cabin, right at the end of the old road. I don't think Blake built it his own self. Somebody took some time building that cabin. It even had a puncheon floor in it. Most of the new shacks up there are just thrown together out of bits and pieces. That one's a real cabin."

I couldn't say anything. I just stood there feeling cold all over and looked at Tom until he started talking again.

"I sort of hinted to Blake that I'd be available to help if he had any trouble keeping order up there, but I already knowed he had a gang of toughs working for him. Three of them were standing out on the porch when I went in the mine office. I thought I recognized one of them from a poster, but I can't be sure. I ain't found the poster yet, but I will. Blake said them rannys were there to keep the peace in the diggings, then he as good as said he didn't want or need no help from me."

My heart sank even more, and it was a struggle for me not to start yelling for Tom to hurry up with his story. I was getting spooked. The more I heard about this mining business the worse it sounded.

When I finally calmed down enough to talk again, I asked Tom outright, "Have you seen Jim Cason around town lately, Sheriff?"

I knew the words came out of my mouth, but my voice sure didn't sound right in my ears. I almost held my breath as I waited for Tom to answer.

"Now you know something, Ken. It's passing strange you should ask me that. I mentioned to Ollie here just the other day, that I ain't seen Jim Cason in town for a long spell. I think it was sometime last fall I seen him."

Dillard turned to his deputy, "Didn't I say that Ollie?"

Ollie straightened up from where he was leaning against the front of the building and nodded his head in agreement. Heck, Ollie always agrees with Tom.

Tom turned back to me and said, "By rights, Jim ought to 'ave been down here early this month buying his spring supplies, don't you reckon?"

Tom didn't wait for me to answer, but kept right on talking.

"I remember Jim was in town in the fall. I think it musta been late September that he was here. At least I know it was some time before the snow started.

"You come in town with him that day, didn't you Ken?"

I nodded my head. I couldn't get a word out to answer him. My throat was stopped up with the awful feeling of dread I got from thinking about what might have happened to Jim.

"Why, that boy's bound to be out of supplies by now." Dillard rambled on. He knotted up his forehead like he almost had a thought then, but if he had one he decided not to share it with me.

This was getting to be too much for me to deal with. I

turned away from the two men and jumped down off the boardwalk. As I walked away, I finally remembered my manners enough to turn back and wave my hand to Sheriff Dillard and Ollie as I rushed across the street.

Rollo seemed content, so I left him standing where he was in front of the mercantile store and hurried along to the land office. This situation was getting scarier by the minute. I'd been going along happy as a fat cow in tall clover, picturing Jim living up there on the mountain. I imagined him snug in his little cabin, just waiting for spring to open up before he came to town. The crazy story Tom Dillard was telling convinced me that this situation needed some serious looking into.

I noticed again that the sidewalk was full of strange faces. Crowds of people were in the mercantile store and the gun shop. Glancing through the doors as I passed, I could see that the clerks in both stores seemed to be frantically busy. One ran right past me to load a big sack on a wagon.

None of the people I passed on the way to the land office were people I knew. That coulda been because I was so busy worrying about what might have happened to Jim Cason that I couldn't hardly see.

The boundaries of Jim Cason's homestead claim are as familiar to me as the beginnings and endings of my own ranch. I helped him drive the stakes in the ground to mark his corners early one spring. That was two years ago.

Jim picked himself out about the prettiest spot in this country to start his place. He's situated almost up to the tree line on the mountain and his claim runs right down to the edge of Shell Lake.

Me and Jim spent more than a month up there last summer, building him a good tight cabin and some furniture to go in it. We even dug us a sawpit so we could ripsaw enough boards to put a puncheon floor in the place. I don't know who hated standing in that pit more, me or Jim.

We didn't stop when we finished off the cabin, either. We set to and built a stout corral for his horses and two good tight sheds to hold his sheep.

Yep, that's right, Jim's planning to run sheep on his place.

Now believe me, I ain't no sheep man. I raise red cows like any sensible man. But that Jim Cason, he's got a bee in his bonnet that he can make himself a fortune up there raising some kind of special breed of sheep. He probably got that notion out of a dratted newspaper. He's almost as bad as Millie Kendrick for reading everything he can get his hands on.

I think Jim mighta said it was some sheep that come over from Spain that he's so het up about raising on his ranch. The last time I talked to him he was all excited. He told me that the kinds of grasses that grow naturally up in those mountain clearings are exactly the sort of grazing that breed of sheep need to eat so they can thrive.

It about broke Jim's daddy's heart to think his only son would turn into a sheep herder, but Jim's so iron-headed that he's got to have his way once an idea takes ahold on him. His daddy's right-smart stuck up to my way of thinking, and the idea that his son would even want to leave his place and start up his own ranch was bad enough, but add the sheep and Major Cason was plumb mortified, I reckon. I know the Major and Jim got into an awful argument, and Jim was so bent out of shape that he swore to me he'd never set foot on his daddy's place again.

When I got in front of the land office I could see Judge Stern through the window. He was sitting there behind his desk with his feet up on a chair, reading a newspaper. The useless old fool. Now, Stern ain't really no judge, he's only the federal land agent, but it sets him up some when folks name him judge.

"How-do Judge," I said as I walked through the door. "How you getting along these days?"

Stern looked up from the paper and eyed me. I watched his expression, but I couldn't read anything, except I thought he was looking a little bit more unfriendly than normal. But that ain't even a little bit of a surprise. He likes to think he's better'n most folks around here.

"Hello there, Kendrick, I'm just fine, thank you."

He stood up as he asked. "What can I do for you today?"

It was possible Stern's voice sounded a little bit odd when he said that, but then it may be that I was looking for something so hard I was just imagining things.

Stepping across the public part of the floor to lean my elbows on the counter I said, "First, I'd like to take a look at the plat book that covers the upper reaches of Shell Mountain, Judge. Then I'll want to see what claims have been filed up there recently."

Stern got a queer look on his face then, and sort of hesitated for just a second. It was clear enough that he didn't want to show me that book. But there was no way he could rightly refuse. He knew I understood the law. That plat book and the survey maps are public property.

Even if Stern came up with enough nerve to actually refuse to let me see the records all I had to do was go get the sheriff and he'd be forced to hand 'em over. He knows that. It took him some time, way longer than it should have, but he finally reached underneath the counter and lifted the big leather book up on top. He even opened it to the right pages.

"If you're planning to go hunting gold up there you're some late, boy." Stern said. I thought he sounded sort of sarcastic like. "You've got to go up on the mountain to the Blake Mining Company office and buy a mining rights claim from them now. That is if Captain Blake has any claims left. All the federal land up there has already been filed on."

Stern was trying to look sort of I-don't-care-like as he

continued talking, so I just stood there and kept staring at him. It was plain enough that something was making him feel uncomfortable.

"I just want to check out the maps and pages that cover Jim Cason's claims." I said. "He filed on his place in the middle of September, I think it was." I kept watching Stern's face as I talked. "Seems like it was around two years ago now. I came in the office with him that day."

"That's right, I remember that you did that." Stern said. I thought his voice was beginning to sound a mite unsteady.

"Kendrick, I know young Cason filed on two pieces of property up there, but he never stayed on the land long enough to prove up on it, so another settler's got the claim on that spot now."

I held on to my temper, but I felt like going across that counter and kicking that low-down, miserable, double-talking varmint right into the middle of next week.

"What the devil do you mean Cason didn't prove up?" I demanded. My voice kept getting louder with every word. "Jim staked his claim, come down here and registered it proper, and built himself a cabin. I know he did all that, Judge, cause I helped him do it. He's been living up there on the property year-round for near-about two years now. That's what the government requires a body to do to prove up on a claim, ain't it?"

"You're wrong about that, Kendrick. You're just wrong. Cason wasn't living up there at all this winter. His cabin and corrals are standing empty and he's long gone. Captain Blake told me it looked to him like Cason had been gone from there since sometime early last fall."

Stern's voice was getting louder too and his eyes began to look sort of blank. It seemed to me like I could feel his lies filling up the little office.

All of a sudden I knew I couldn't stand still for Stern's weaseling another minute. I reached over the counter to

grab hold of his arm and yanked him over close to me. I
jerked him as hard as I could too. I wanted to make darn
sure he felt it.

"Exactly what is it you're trying to tell me." I was so
mad by then that my words almost sounded like a snarl.

Stern tried to pull his arm out of my grip, but he wasn't
strong enough. His face turned about as white as butcher's
paper and he almost screamed, "Take your hands off me,
you crazy hoodlum. I'll call the sheriff."

"You know I ain't worried none about Tom Dillard. Go
ahead and call him if you want to. He needs to know about
this, same as me. If I remember rightly, he's one of Jim
Cason's good friends, just like I am. He'd be more like to
side with me than to pay any mind to anything you've got
to say Stern, and you know it."

I yanked on his arm again and almost pulled his sorry
behind all the way across the counter.

"You talk to me."

My temper was so fired up it felt like I was almost spitting the words out through my teeth when I said that.

Giving Stern another stiff shake, I thought how much he
reminded me of a sneaking coward of a coyote. What I
really wanted to do was punch his lying face in for him. A
terrible, sick feeling was telling me that Jim Cason was
almost sure to be dead—that maybe he'd been dead for a
month or more by now. That feeling about filled me up
with rage.

There was no way Jim would simply walk off and leave
his place, not after all the work we had put in on it. Building that ranch was Jim's dream. He just wouldn't leave it.
Not for no more time than it would take for him to make
a trip to town for supplies or maybe to go visit his sister.

I stuck my face right down in front of Stern's ugly, lying
mug and said. "You tell me what you know about that
Blake Mining Company."

He sort of shriveled up then, like he might faint or something, and started in to whining. "All I know about it is a stranger that called himself Captain Malcolm Blake came in here about six weeks ago and showed me a hand-drawn map of the land up at the top of the mountain. He said he wanted to file a claim on the land that runs all the way around Shell Lake. I told him another claim was recorded right in the middle of what he wanted. That's when he explained that he had found the mountain deserted. Then he filled out the paperwork to file on the land."

"And you accepted his filing right over-top of Jim Cason's, just like that? You didn't think you needed some sort of proof besides that man's word?"

My temper seemed to be getting worse every time I spoke a word.

"You'd take the word of some stranger you never seen before against a hometown boy you've known since he was a youngster? Without even checking it out or anything? Didn't you think the man could be lying?" Every time I asked a question I gave Stern a hard shake.

"I can't be running ten miles up on top of a mountain to check on every homestead somebody comes in here and says they find deserted. I've got this office to run." Stern was almost crying.

His whining aggravated me so I shoved him back across the counter. I pushed him so hard he fell on the floor with his back leaning up against his desk.

"You'll find out what you can and can't do after I ride out and tell Major Cason what you done with his son's claim."

Staring down at the whimpering coward, I felt so spiteful I couldn't keep from adding, "I hope that stranger paid you enough money to get your no-account behind out of town before the Major gets his hands on you. I'm on my way out to his place right now to tell him what you've done."

I turned around and stomped out into the street. It may be I was mad enough right that minute to kill somebody with my bare hands. I sure felt like I was. If that blasted skunk Stern woulda been worth it I'd a liked to start out on him. On top of that I was feeling almost crazy with fear over what might have happened to Jim.

Chapter Two

Almost running, I went down the street to the bank. Rushing in the door, I cashed the draft for the ranch payroll money and barely nodded to the clerk. That draft was the real reason I had come to town in the first place. I came out of the bank and hotfooted it back across the street to jump on Rollo. It took me a while, and I fussed and fumed at the delay without making a whit of difference, but I finally worked my way through the crowded street to the edge of town and headed straight out to Major Cason's ranch.

The Casons' came here and bought out an old timer's spread that's located about five miles south of town. It's right along the road to my place. I pass by the entrance every time I come to town. I must have been about ten years old when they started their ranch. The land they bought meets up with our place where it runs along the banks of the San Luis River.

Josh Wilkins, the old timer that built the place, come into the country the same time my father and mother did. I was born not too long after, but I don't really remember anything about how hard it was on them the first few years they were here. Of course I've heard plenty of stories about

how those men had to work to chase out Indians and outlaws and to make their homes here.

Momma used to love to talk about those times. The stories she told seemed almost like fairy tales to me. She made
Dad and his friend Josh sound bigger than life. They were
real-live heroes to her. When I think about how her stories
made us young ones look up to him I don't wonder that
Dad's heart give out after Momma died.

Major Cason came in and built his ranch up to be a real
showplace in no time at all. He runs a herd of mixed cattle
and raises Morgan horses. I think it must be a pretty big
operation. I've heard that he keeps more than thirty men
on his payroll, what with his horse trainers and regular
riders and all.

Being as we was such close neighbors, and the only boys
anywhere near our age for miles around, Jim Cason and
me got to be good friends right away. We both loved to
fish the creeks and hunt the woods and meadows up on the
mountains. It wasn't hardly no time at all until we was
almost like brothers. We've been that way ever since.

I think sometimes Jim could be a mite sweet on Millie,
but that's just me supposing. He ain't never said anything
to me about it though and neither has Millie. I did notice
that Jim came over to eat supper at our house a lot last
summer.

I've often felt a little bit like I ought to go around to the
back door since Major Cason's house is so fine. But I didn't
even stop to think about such a thing this time. I'd worked
myself up into such a lather I wasn't thinking about much
at all except that something so bad had happened to Jim
that it couldn't be fixed.

Leaving Rollo ground tied, I ran up the front steps to the
porch and yanked on the bell rope a couple of times. In a
few minutes I heard heavy footsteps rush down the hall and
Major Cason himself pulled the door open.

Now the Major's quite a figure. He's every bit as tall as

I am and big with it, but he's strong as a bull. His hair and mustache are gone solid white, but he's a handsome old devil.

"Wayne Kendrick." He was talking in a really friendly, welcoming voice I'd never heard him use before.

He smiled and continued on, "It's good to see you, boy." He held out his hand to me like I was his long lost friend.

The way he was acting really threw me there for a minute. Major Cason ain't never had all that much use for me. The last time I saw the man I was on the street in Belden. It was one day early this past winter. I was in town getting some supplies.

He stood right there on the boardwalk and cussed me something disgraceful. He was fighting mad at me for helping Jim build his cabin and corrals so he could prove up on his homestead.

My hand sort of automatically lifted itself up and shook the hand the major was sticking out at me, but I kept on watching his face. I was so dogged busy trying to figure out what in blazes was going on with the man I couldn't think of a darn thing to say for a second or two.

Still smiling a big fake-looking smile, Cason kept right on talking, "I was telling Margaret Rose just the other day that we hadn't seen you or Millie in months, Ken. Is your ranch keeping you so busy since your father died that you can't even spare the time to come visit your friends?"

I still couldn't understand the way the man was acting and talking, so I decided to ignore his craziness and came right out with what I wanted to say.

"Look here, Major, I rode out here to see you for a purpose. Have you heard anything from Jim in the last few weeks?"

His face went sort of pale then and all of a sudden he was looking like he couldn't meet my eyes. I thought he showed about the sneakiest look on his face I had ever seen on anybody. His voice sounded real strained when he answered me too, like he was having trouble getting the words out.

"Why no, Ken, I haven't heard a word from Jim for a while. You know how he's been. He's so determined to stay up on that mountain with those infernal sheep of his and prove he can make it on his own that he hasn't been home in months."

"There's a bit of a problem with that, Major."

I was feeling downright bitter, considering what I had learned from the Sheriff and Julius Stern. I'm sure it showed in my voice.

"Jim's not up on the mountain at all. Some unknown sidewinder that goes by the name of Captain Malcolm Blake come down to Belden claiming he found Jim's cabin and corrals deserted. That low-down skunk of a Julius Stern let the fella file his claim right over top of Jim's. All this happened a good three or four weeks back. Stern knew better, but he went ahead and did the paper work for the man anyway. I accused him of accepting a bribe to do the filing, and he couldn't deny it."

"You're saying Jim's not up on Shell Mountain? Well of course he's up there. Where else would he be? I find that strange, to say the least. I'm sure someone's mistaken about that."

Major Cason sure wasn't no actor. His voice sounded kind of hollow as he babbled on and on. His problem was the same one a lot of people have when they try to lie. He's so used to telling the truth all the time that all he managed to do was to sound and look exactly like he was lying.

While Major Cason was trying to figure out what to say next and how to go about saying it, Meg, or Margaret Rose as the Major calls her, opened a door and stepped out into the hallway.

Her shiny black hair was hanging loose down her back. My heart started to pounding. It's awful hard for me to get my breath when I get up real close to her. It's been like that ever since she got to be about sixteen and the Major stopped her from following Jim and me around all the time.

Meg stopped for a minute and stared when she saw me standing there in the front doorway talking to her father. Then she came rushing down the hall to where the Major and me were standing.

Meg stopped when she got beside her father. They exchanged a look that seemed sort of strange to me. I thought the expression on her face made her look about as guilty as the Major was looking.

"Hello Ken, what was that you just told Dad about Jim?" Meg asked, as she turned to me.

She stepped over close to the door and was smiling up at me so pretty I almost lost my train of thought there for a minute. Now that seemed strange to me too. She's been acting like I was something that crawled up out of a crack in front of her father ever since she come home from the East.

Every time I've been over here and asked after her, either Jim or her daddy have made some excuse about her being too busy to entertain. At first I wondered if Meg had finally decided she didn't have any use for me any more. But then I sort of got the idea that maybe it was Jim and the Major. It's possible they acted the same way to any man that showed an interest in Meg. I been thinking lately that maybe they just don't want to lose their cook and house-keeper.

I couldn't help but notice that her sweet brown eyes were all swollen up like she'd been crying some though, and her face was kinda red.

"Excuse me, Meg." I got over my shock at this strange new friendliness of hers and grabbed my hat to hold it down by my side. I tried to ask my question again.

"Maybe you can help me. I was just trying to find out from your Pa here if you all had heard anything from Jim since last fall?"

Meg looked me up and down like she was trying to weigh up whether or not I could be trusted. She didn't answer right away. She turned away from me a little and stood there looking down at the floor for a second. There was a puzzled look on her face. I sure didn't know what was going on, but she waited long enough for me to get to feeling a little bit impatient with her.

She finally turned her face back toward me. Her voice sounded as strained as her Pa's had when she said, "Ken, Jim's been kidnapped."

"What?"

"He's been kidnapped."

I didn't know whether to be glad to hear her say that or to be scared worse than I already was. I felt just plain stumped. I couldn't think of a thing to say or do for a minute.

I stepped over the threshold and into the hallway to stand close to Meg. When I put my hand on her shoulder I could feel her trembling through my glove.

About that time Major Cason set in to yelling at Meg like he was some kind of a madman. "You promised you wouldn't open your mouth about that to anyone, girl. Why in the devil did you have to tell him?"

Meg's face went redder than it was before. She looked hurt and tears came up in her eyes. She held her head up high though, and surprised the heck out of me by yelling right back at the Major.

"I don't care what you think, Papa. I know my brother, even if you don't. Kendrick is Jim's best friend. He would want Ken to know what's going on. He would trust him to help us, too."

"Those crooks warned us that if we told anybody anything they'd put a bullet in Jim's head and dump his body on our front porch. Your loose tongue may have just killed your brother."

The Major's words were pure cruelty, but they were a

cry of pain. He loved his only son above all things. I've always believed he loved Jim above his daughter. I'm sure he loves him above his ranch. If the truth was known, he probably loves Jim more than he ever loved his wife who died when Meg was born. I couldn't help but think what he had just said to Meg proved that was true.

Still shaken by the news that there was a possibility Jim was still alive, I started thinking again. Back in town, when I heard Stern say that Jim's claim and his cabin and the other things he worked so hard for were sitting up there abandoned, and had been taken over by that Malcolm Blake, I was seriously scared for him. I didn't want to admit it to myself, but I had made sure in my mind that Jim was dead.

"Major," I said quietly, fighting to contain my excitement and the feeling of hope that washed over me. "It's no good for you to yell at Meg. Please tell me what's going on here. Maybe I can help."

"The best thing you can do for Jim is to get the devil out of here and keep your blasted mouth shut about this," he said nastily, drawing himself up straight and trying to stare me down.

Suddenly he sounded normal to me. The Major always was a prideful so and so. I knew the man was distraught over his son, but I was about to get down right irritated with him.

"It's like this, Major Cason, you can just make up your mind that I ain't gonna do anything of the kind," I said that flatly, looking him right in the eyes. "I'm gonna stand right here in your hallway until you tell me everything or I'm going to ride straight up to Shell Mountain and figure it out for myself."

The Major's shoulders drooped. He suddenly looked like an old, broken man. He turned his back to me then, and walked down the hallway toward his office without saying a word.

I thought at first he was going to simply walk out on us, but he swung around to look back at me and Meg when he reached the office door. He waved his hand to motion for us to follow him. When we got inside the office he was slumped down in the chair behind his desk and holding his head in his hands.

"You tell him Meg," he said. "Get the letter those devils left here and let Kendrick read it for himself."

Meg rushed over to a tall oak cabinet and yanked open the bottom drawer. Taking out a flat leather case, she opened it and pulled out a grubby piece of folded paper and came back across the room to hand it to me.

"This note was left here sometime night before last, Ken. Papa found it stuck under the front door when he got up yesterday morning."

Unfolding the paper, I read, "We have your son. Get $10,000.00 in small bank notes. Wait for instructions. If you tell anyone about this or go to the law, we'll put a bullet in your son's head and dump his body on your front porch."

There was no signature. The paper and the handwriting looked crude, but that didn't necessarily mean anything. It was probably deliberately done that way to hide who it was that wrote it.

The first thing to do was figure out who was doing this. We had to know that before we could hold out any hope of helping Jim. I read the letter over a couple more times, hoping I would recognize the way the person made his letters if I ever saw the writing again, then I handed it back to Meg.

"Have you heard any more from them?" I asked.

"No," she said, shaking her head. "Not a word."

"Do you have any idea who it could be?"

"Papa and I have thought and thought, but we can't think of anyone who could do this."

Meg started to cry in earnest then. She hid her face in

her hands for a minute then she looked back up—right into my eyes. Tears were still running down her cheeks.

She put one of her little hands up on my chest and talked right through her crying, "Please find him, Ken. Please."

She turned away then and ran past me to go out of the room. I felt so bad for her that I prayed I'd be able to get my hands around the neck of the lowdown snake that wrote that awful note.

"Major, I'm sorry to push you, but I need to know some things before I leave here." I was ready to do something, if I could figure out anything to do that might really help Jim. "How do you know that Jim's really alive?"

The major didn't answer that, so I kept on asking. "Have you gotten any other messages that Meg doesn't know about?"

The look on Cason's face made me feel lower than ever.

He dropped his head and covered his face with his hands again. His voice was muffled, but I could hear him.

"I don't know that Jim's alive, Ken."

He lifted his head again to look at me, his voice breaking. There were tears on his cheeks, too.

"Meg believes he's still alive, Ken. I just don't know."

"Can you get the money they asked for?"

"That's a dumb question for you to ask me." He sort of sputtered in disgust and gave me a hard look.

"I got the money together the second day after those crooks left that ransom note. I had to send riders all the way over to the county seat as well as to the bank in Belden, but I've got it ready and waiting. I'd have that money if I had to mortgage the ranch and sell all my stock, you should know that."

"Well, I'm sure you'll go ahead and do whatever they say to do about the money if they contact you again." I was talking a little absently, thinking hard on a plan for what I might do to help. "Major Cason, I'm going up to Shell Mountain and act like I'm one of those gold hunters that are flocking up there. That way I'll be able to check around and see if I can find out anything about where Jim could be without anybody getting suspicious about what I'm up to."

The Major straightened up and scowled at me then. His eyes were dark and he looked twenty years older than he had when he opened his front door a few minutes before.

"For God's sake be careful, Ken. If you tip your hand that you know about this kidnapping note those men will kill Jim for sure, if they haven't already done it."

"Major, something's got to be done. We can't just sit here on our hands. We've got to make some effort to find Jim. If you pay those crooks the money they're asking you for, what's to keep them from going ahead and putting a bullet through Jim's head as soon as they get their hands on it? I've got to try to find out something, you know that."

I kept my voice down, trying to sound a little softer toward him. The Major aggravated the devil out of me. He always had. But my heart ached for the old man. He looked to be about at the end of his rope.

"I guess you're right."

Cason hesitated again, then he added.

"Doggone it, Ken, of course you're right. We can't just sit on our hands. You take care up there. Don't let anything happen to you. Please let us know something as quick as you can. Margaret Rose and I are both about crazy with worry over that boy."

He walked closer and held out his hand, "Thank you, son. Please find Jim and bring him home safe for us."

When I left the Major's house I jumped back on Rollo and pushed him hard toward Belden. I kept thinking as fast as I could, trying to come up with a realistic plan to find out what happened to Jim.

I still felt about scared to death every time my thoughts went around to what all could be happening to him. When my thoughts went that way I tried to force myself not to think about anything but finding him safe.

As important as Jim is to me, every other minute it seemed like I would have to shake my head to keep from thinking about Meg instead. I kept reliving the deep feeling of joy that hit me when Meg's hand touched my chest and she looked up and asked me to help her.

Riding all the way back to my ranch to get the supplies I would need to pretend to be a miner was out of the question. It was much too far. It just wouldn't do for me to take the time to make the trip. If there was the barest chance that Jim was still alive I couldn't be waiting around. I would have to get up on the mountain as fast as I could and start trying to find out something.

By the time I got back to Belden, I'd decided to go ahead and use the payroll money I got from the bank as a stake. It was more than enough to buy the supplies and gear I would need to set myself up as a miner. I allowed to myself that my ranch hands would surely wait around another week or two to get their pay before they quit and walked off on me.

The first place I stopped when I got back to town was Southwood's mercantile. The store was still crowded when I walked in, and I noticed that there were two men clerking that must be newcomers to Belden. At least I didn't recognize them. I was hoping I would get one of those men to wait on me, but when it came my turn I was unlucky and ended up having to read my list out to Mrs. Southwood, the storekeeper's wife.

She came over to the counter where I was standing and asked me what I needed. When I read off what supplies I wanted she just stood there and stared at me like she thought I had gone off the deep end or something.

Mrs. Southwood finally stopped gawking at me and picked up a sack to begin getting the things together I asked for. I guess her curiosity just plain got the best of her finally though. She turned around all of a sudden to give me a hard look and sort of marched back over to the counter.

"Wayne Allan Kendrick, what in the world do you think you're doing now?" She whispered it like it was too shameful for folks to hear her.

I guess I answered her a little bit too sharp for politeness.

"What in blazes does it look like I'm doing? I'm getting ready to go up on Shell Mountain like everybody else around here. I'm gonna see if I can't dig me up some of the gold that's supposed to be up there."

She looked kind of insulted and stuck her nose right up in the air. With about the coldest voice you ever heard in your life she said, "You've got no call to speak to me like that, young man."

I don't reckon I did look or sound none too friendly. Mrs. Southwood was like most people around Belden. She's known me all my life, and even though I'm well over thirty years old and getting some gray on the sides of my head Mrs. Southwood and a lot of other people don't seem to see any change in me. Some still act like I'm a little kid with a couple of teeth out in front that they need to help mind.

"I apologize for speaking so sharp, Mrs. Southwood," I said, trying to sound as humble as I could. "I didn't mean to snap at you, and I'm sorry to sound so impatient, but I'm in an awful hurry."

She made a snorting sound, or whatever you call it when a lady blows air out of her nose like that, but she didn't say anything else. She finished getting my order together and slammed the bill down on the counter, dipping the pen in the inkpot and holding it out for me to use to sign the bill.

I ignored the pen she was trying to hand me and counted out the cash money to pay her. It surely wouldn't do for me to charge the order to the ranch account. When I glanced up I noticed that Mrs. Southwood had finally stopped looking like she wanted to bite my head off. I reckon she felt a heap better about me going a little crazy if I paid her cash for my supplies.

I left my stuff at the store where it would be safe and went out on the street to lead Rollo around to the livery barn. When I got there I dropped Rollo's reins over the door of an empty stall and yelled to the stableman as I stuck my head in the door of his little office.

"Hey Jake, I need a wagon or a buckboard right away."

Jake Ellis, the livery stable owner, tipped his chair back and laughed out loud, right in my face. I couldn't keep from feeling a little miffed. He didn't simply laugh, he kept right on hooting. I wondered if I should tell him how much he sounded like a braying jackass.

"What the heck is so blasted funny about that?"

"Ken, oh Ken. You're about as simple as one of those pilgrims that keep crowding in here trying to get themselves equipped to go up on Shell Mountain to scrape for gold. Heck boy, there's not a wagon or anything to substitute for a wagon left within twenty miles of this town. Every wagon, buggy, buckboard, or cart anywhere around here has been bought up by those gold-crazy immigrants."

Jake's a big, white-haired, red-faced German. Most folks figure he musta been a schoolteacher once or something like that. He talks so high-falutin he always sounds out of place. I think he just learned his English out of a book.

"Then hitch Miss Hetty's grays to her buckboard for me," I said, speaking just as reasonable as I could.

His eyebrows shot up then and he grabbed his belly with both hands and started up that doggoned crazy laughing of his again. When he finally stopped and caught his breath, he said, "I think you've gone completely off your rocker today, boy. Nobody, and I mean nobody, touches those

gray geldings without Miss Hetty Kendrick's express per-
mission. I don't care if you are her only nephew, you're
not going to touch them either."

I was beginning to get just about all I wanted of that
"boy" stuff. Me and Jake Ellis never have hit it off too
good anyhow. He's held some hard feelings toward me ever
since me and some of the boys around town got ourselves
a little liquored up one night and went looking for some
fun. We ended up taking Jake's best wagon apart and putting it back together up on the roof of his livery stable.
That trick wouldn't a been so awful bad by itself, I don't
reckon, except that the only fellas Jake could find to hire
to get his wagon apart and down off the roof again was me
and the boys that put it up there in the first place.

Well, that all happened near about ten years ago, maybe
even more, and Jake still holds it against me. It don't help
much that most of the men in town think it's one of the
best stories they ever heard and tell it over and over again
right regular.

I could see that I wasn't going to get any willing coop-
eration out of Jake without giving him some kind of serious
encouragement. I didn't have any patience left at all, so I
slipped my .44 out of my holster and let it kinda dangle
down in my left hand.

"Go get that buckboard hitched up, Jake," I said, keeping
my voice nice and quiet. "I'll take full responsibility for it
and explain everything to Miss Hetty. I don't have time for
this."

Jake opened his mouth again, but I stared at him, and
for some reason he seemed to think better of whatever it
was he was planning to say. He gave me a couple of hard
looks, but he shut his mouth and walked over to one of the
stalls and started throwing a harness on one of the geldings.

Maybe I looked a lot meaner than I realized. I stood there
being quiet and holding the gun in my hand until Jake was

finished harnessing the team, then I followed him outside and watched as he backed the horses up to Miss Hetty's fancy, two-seated buckboard. By that time I was starting to think he would never get finished, but he finally worked the grays into position and hooked their singletrees to the buckboard's doubletree and the rig was ready to go.

"I'll bring the buckboard and the horses back in a few days, Jake." I said as I climbed up on the seat. "My reason for doing this is important, but I can't take the time to explain it to you right now. Take good care of my horse for me."

Anybody could have seen that Jake was getting so mad that he couldn't keep his mouth shut any longer. "You can be sure you'll explain this, you bullying young scoundrel. You're much too old to get away with pranks like this. I don't care if you are one of the jumped-up Kendricks. I know you've always been as wild as a March hare, but you cannot be allowed to take anything you want at gunpoint. I'll swear a warrant out on you for this. Taking this rig this way is the same as committing armed robbery."

I began to think Jake sounded mighty-near hysterical. His cheeks were turning bright red he was so puffed up with fury. I figured that as soon as I was out of his sight he'd go running around town tattling to Miss Hetty and Tom Dillard. Probably he'd go to both of them.

"Just go on back in your office and stay there and be quiet for a few minutes, Jake."

I made it a point to gently wave the pistol around a little as I placed it beside me on the seat of the buckboard. It seemed important to make sure Jake could still see it. I smiled down at him as I guided the buckboard past where he was standing and turned out the corral gate into the alley. Jake looked so mad by the time I went past him that I had to wonder what it would look like if he exploded.

Slowly guiding the team back through the crowded

streets, I finally got it parked in front of the mercantile and rushed inside to pick up my supplies. It took me four trips to load it all.

Southwood himself was in the front of the store then, but he didn't even offer to help me load my things. I reckon his wife had been talking to him. He just stood there like a stick and stared at me. I ignored him. As soon as I got everything stowed in the back of the buckboard I jumped up on the seat again and left town.

The only way to move along the street was to sort of force my way through all the pilgrims. It wasn't easy going. When I finally reached a clear road I lifted the reins and pushed the grays until they were running flat out. A few hundred yards from town I turned the team off the main road to splash through the ford at Taylor's Creek and cut across the pasture to Aunt Hetty's house.

I knew Hetty Kendrick was the one person around that I could tell about Jim and trust not to pass it on to everybody in town. She'd stop anybody from looking for me too, if that fool of a Jake Ellis really did go so far as to take out a warrant on me. When I got close to her house I slowed down enough to wheel the buckboard around to the back and pulled up near the steps to the porch.

About the time my boots hit the ground Miss Hetty screeched at me through the kitchen window, "What in blue blazes do you think you're doing with my rig, you ornery little polecat?"

I grinned as I walked up the steps to cross the porch and enter the kitchen, letting the outside door slam shut behind me. Miss Hetty's another one of those people that still thinks of me as if I was about nine or ten years old and up to some trick or another all the time.

They all need to stop and take a good look. If I'm anything at all I sure ain't little. My shirts have to be tailor made so I don't rip them out at the shoulders when I'm working, and I can only wear these special-made boots. It ain't that my feet are so awful big or anything. They're just long like the rest of me.

Miss Hetty was standing in the middle of her kitchen floor when I stepped through the door. She had her hands stuck on her hips and I could see she was struggling to look like she was mad, but I knew her. She was really having trouble keeping a grin off her face.

"What the devil do you think you're playing at, boy?" she asked, still trying her best to sound angry.

I picked her up and kissed her before she could start up to talking again. Miss Hetty is my Pa's big sister and I don't know her full story exactly, but there's some sort of mystery about her.

I don't figure anybody knows all the ins and outs of it since Pa died except maybe Hetty herself. That woman learned some tough, independent ways somewhere or another. Pa used to say Hetty didn't need to learn anything about being hard to deal with, that she was born stubborn and independent and just got worse as she got older.

"Calm yourself down now, sweetheart," I said, hugging her tight. "It's all in a good cause, I promise you. Fix me some of that coffee that smells so good and make me a sandwich, please? I'll sit down here and tell you all about everything."

"Well drat your hide anyway, you little scamp of misery, you steal my rig and ride in here driving my horses like a madman and still have the nerve to ask me to feed you?" She was over by the stove filling a coffee cup while she fussed.

I sat down at the big table in the center of the kitchen sipping on the coffee and watched her as she sliced bread and ham to make two big sandwiches.

Hetty's tiny, but she's a presence. Her snow-white hair is always blowing around her face, but one look at her sparkly blue eyes and that's all you ever see.

She slapped a plate down in front of me and snapped,

"now will you tell me what the heck is happening before I get mad at you?"

I swallowed about half of the first sandwich before I stopped chewing long enough to say, "Jim Cason disappeared, Hetty. I'm headed up to Shell Mountain to try and find out what's going on."

Hetty dropped down into a chair across the table from me. She was suddenly all business and her face was full of her concern for Jim. She knew how close Jim Cason and I had always been, and I knew she was right fond of Jim her own self. Hetty was also the only person who knew how I felt about Meg Cason. Her face paled as she read the seriousness in my expression.

"What in the world is going on, son?"

"Jim's in serious trouble. That's what's going on. The Major found a letter on his porch yesterday morning that said he should get a bunch of money ready to trade for Jim. I'm afraid it's possible he's been killed by now. It's clear something serious has happened to him. I just don't know exactly what it is yet. From what I've been hearing, he's been missing from his claim for several weeks. Julius Stern told me that this morning. I made up my mind then that Jim had to be dead. Stern said some stranger named Malcolm Blake told him that Jim's claim was abandoned. I knew that wasn't right. I was afraid the only way Jim's claim could be deserted was for him to be dead. When I rode out to the Major's place to tell him about what Stern said he and Meg told me about the ransom demand. Whoever wrote the note said they were holding Jim prisoner. They wanted the money or they threatened to shoot Jim and throw his body on the Major's porch. The note told the Major to get ten thousand dollars ready and wait for instructions on how to pay it over."

"Lord help us, what is this world coming to?" Hetty said, shaking her head in amazement.

"I'm going up to the mining camp to nose around and

see what I can find out. I need your rig so I can pretend to
be one of the gold hunters. That way I'll have a good excuse to be up there, and I can look around without tipping
my hand. My hope is that I can nose around and find out
where the kidnappers are keeping Jim. If he ain't dead yet,
that is. I'm afraid whoever it is that kidnapped him will go
ahead and kill him and get rid of his body as soon as the
Major pays over the money they're demanding."

Miss Hetty put one of her hands on each side of her face
and asked. "What can I do to help, Ken?"

There never was a doubt in my mind that she'd react
exactly like that. Hetty's always been my trump card when
I get myself in a jam.

"Let me take the geldings and your rig. Then make sure
nobody's trying to find me for two or three days."

It seemed like a good time to warn her about the trouble
coming her way so I kept talking, "Old Jake Ellis got his
tail feathers some ruffled a while ago. He was downright
put out with me when I made him give me your horses and
buckboard. He got so blasted hard for me to deal with when
I asked for them that I felt forced to draw my pistol to
encourage him to cooperate. He swore he was going to take
out a warrant on me for armed robbery."

Hetty chuckled, her blue eyes dancing. "Lord, Ken, how
I would have loved to see Jake Ellis' fat old face when you
did that. I'll bet that pompous old coot hustled over to Tom
Dillard's office before you got clear of town. You know
he'll be out here whining to me before nightfall. He has
reason to know what he's facing when I get mad. We've
had our differences before this. So he's scared. Money is
Jake's god, you know, and he doesn't want me to lay the
blame on him if anything happens to my horses or the
buckboard."

"I'll bet you're exactly right about that," I answered,
laughing at her delight in Jake Ellis' discomfort.

Pushing my chair back from the table I stood up. "I'm

going to hit the road on up to the mountain. It would be good if I could get up there and get myself settled in a campsite somewhere before it's completely dark tonight. If Jake and the sheriff come out here looking to arrest me you'll head them off, won't you?"

"You bet I will. I'll ask that thickheaded Tom Dillard what the blazes he means by chasing my nephew around the country. I'll act all upset and threaten to sue him if he doesn't leave you alone. That'll get him so confused I guarantee you he'll forget all about chasing after you. He'll have to think about it for several days before he does anything else, at the very least."

Leaning over to hug her again I went out back to climb in the buckboard. Miss Hetty followed me down the steps and settled a covered basket over in the back alongside my supplies.

I looked back across the fields toward town before I took out, but I couldn't see any riders coming. Maybe Tom Dillard wasn't so thickheaded as we thought he was. I've noticed that most men have enough sense to stay well clear of Hetty Kendrick, especially when she's apt to be a little out of tune.

Touching the geldings' fat rumps with the whip I hurried them on around the house to Hetty's front lane. A few minutes later I picked up the shale road that runs up the mountain. The buckboard bounced along in the ruts and chuckholes that filled the road from ditch to ditch. I guess ruts and other damage are normal with so many people going back and forth to the gold field in heavy wagons.

The horses ran like they were glad to be out of the stable. They moved easily, and didn't seem to notice when the grade began to get steep.

Chapter Three

It was almost dark when I pulled into the mining camp. The first thing I noticed was the white looking tops of tents that were set up all around the place. Toward the back of the open area, grubby-looking little shacks dotted the place where Jim's corrals had been. Most of them looked to have been thrown together out of scrap lumber.

The stand of black spruce that used to grow behind the corrals was gone. I couldn't see anything left but the stumps. The trees might have been chopped down for firewood or maybe they were used for timbers in the little one-man mines the gold hunters make.

I shivered when I thought about those shafts. Thinking about those little holes in the ground about gives me the shudders. The miners call those little tunnels they dig into the side of a hill "tipples." They're plain old holes in the dirt to me, and they look almighty dangerous.

I've always figured they'd be sure to come right down on top of a man. Several times in my life I've sworn that I wouldn't go inside one of those dratted, scary places for any amount of money. Now I suddenly realized it might be necessary for me to go in one for no pay at all, if I was serious about passing myself off as a gold miner.

Somebody had nailed a big sign up over the door of the little cabin. Blake Mining Company was painted across it in big black letters. That sight didn't help my temper none. Jim and me took extra special care building that cabin because we was expecting it to be his home.

I was beginning to look forward to getting to know that Captain Blake gent in a impolite sort of way. I kept thinking about maybe punching his face in or even shooting him in the leg.

Easing the buckboard into the open space in front of the cabin I tied the team to the hitch rail. There didn't appear to be anybody hanging about right at that minute, but there's always a bit of thievery going on in a place like this where there's lots of strangers moving around. I wanted the rig and my supplies up close where I could keep my eye on them.

I jumped down from the buckboard and climbed up on the cabin porch. I had to duck my head to walk in the door. The first thing I noticed was a partition that was nailed up from end to end to divide the cabin into two rooms. The front part, the part I was standing in, had a long counter and some maps nailed up on the wall behind it. The room was empty.

My boot heels sounded kind of loud on the puncheon floor. About a minute later a young woman stepped out of the back room and came over to the counter. She had light-colored hair that was a pretty color, but she had it skinned straight back away from her face and tied with a piece of string. She was wearing an ugly brown-colored shirt that dangled loose over a pair of miner's pants. Her boots made almost as much noise hitting the floor as mine did.

The woman's voice sounded younger than she looked. "Can I help you with something, mister?"

Yanking my hat off, I sort of bowed before I answered her. That seemed to embarrass her for some reason.

She got kind of pink and irritated looking and spoke

again, sounding sort of impatient, "What do you want, mister?"

"Excuse me for troubling you, Miss, but could I see Mr. Blake?"

"Mr. Blake isn't here at the moment. You'll have to do business with me." Her chin went up and she made her voice sound sort of stern.

Well, you can bet that surprised me some. Just imagine a young woman like that running a mining business, all by herself. And if what I was thinking panned out to be true, it was going to prove out to be a crooked mining business. When I thought of that it was my turn to feel a little embarrassed.

I finally got my tongue loosened up enough so I could say, "I want to buy me a claim, please Ma'am."

She gave me what I thought was a sort of disgusted look and said, "All the gold claims we had are already sold. If you get one now you'll have to buy it directly from one of the miners who want to leave the diggings."

As soon as she said that she turned away from the counter and started for the door to the back room.

"Hey, wait a minute," I yelled, leaning over the counter.

She stopped by the door to the back room and turned to look over toward me. The light from the window caught her full in the face then and I could see that she was sort of good looking. I don't reckon you could say she was pretty exactly, she just had a nice looking, open sort of face, with big, dark eyes and a sweet, pouty looking mouth. It was hard for me to believe that someone so young knew anything about any crooked business like kidnapping Jim Cason.

"Could you maybe steer me to somebody who's in the market to sell his claim, Ma'am?" I kept my voice soft and tried to sound as friendly as possible.

The girl looked at me like she was trying to figure me out. I guess I do look a whole lot more like a cowman than

I do like a miner. She finally stopped staring and answered me.

"There's a man by name of Hal Stinson that's got a claim over on the far-west side of the lake. He was in here early today saying he'd like to sell out so he could go home. He was telling some story about he had a sick wife and some children so he couldn't stay away from home too long. I don't know exactly what kind of a claim he's got over there mister, but you could go talk to him."

"How can I find him?"

"Just keep on going around the lake the way you're already headed. You can tell Stinson's place easy by his wagon. It's got a yellow canvas top."

Thanking her, I headed back out to the buckboard. When I'd been up here last fall helping Jim, the only way to get around the lake was on horseback, but now I could see somebody had marked out a poor excuse for a road that led around to the west.

Climbing up on the seat of the buckboard again I shook the reins along the back of the geldings. They started following the track toward the lake. Pretty soon Miss Hetty's pretty gray horses were getting splashed with mud all the way up to their withers and the buckboard was plumb covered in it.

When I got near-bout halfway around the lake, I finally spotted the yellow-topped wagon the young woman mentioned. It was bright colored enough to gleam a little through the dim light. A tall, thin man was standing over a campfire set about halfway between the wagon and the lake. I figured he had to be the miner the woman told me about.

Pulling the team off the track, I worked the buckboard up close to the man's camp and hailed him.

"Evening, would you be Hal Stinson?"

I couldn't see his face too well. He held his head down and mostly hid it under his hat brim. I noticed that he held his right hand down by his side. It looked to me like he was holding a rifle. He glanced up at me a couple of times and finally answered. He sounded like he was mad about something.

"I'm Stinson, what's your business?"

He sure didn't have manners. In this part of the country folks with a campfire and a hot coffeepot are sort of obliged to ask strangers to get down and join in.

I answered him back in kind.

"I was told you had a gold claim to sell. Do you?"

His head snapped up then so I could see his face. He didn't look near as mean as he had sounded, just kind of sort of tired and a little caved in, like he had maybe given up on life for some reason.

"Are you buying?" he asked.

"Well, I don't know yet, but I might be, if the deal is right."

Stinson surely came alive then. He walked over to rest the barrel of his rifle against the wagon wheel. I noticed he still had a handgun in a holster hanging on his hip. Now that ain't a bit unusual to see in this area—excepting Stinson's a miner.

Most all cattlemen wear guns. There's lots of uses for a hand gun on a ranch, what with having to deal with snakes and wild animals and all, but it's a known fact that mighty few miners ever wear a pistol.

"Get down and sit," Stinson said, finally beginning to act a little bit friendly. "I've got some ripe coffee here and there's some biscuits and beans left over from my supper. You're more'n welcome to 'em."

It seemed like to me that the only polite thing to do then was to overlook his changeableness for the time being, so I got down. I set a rock on the reins so the grays would stand and went over to the fire.

"I'd sure be obliged to eat me some hot food. It's a long ride up that hill and it gets cold come sundown."

Stinson sort of grunted and squatted down beside the fire
to pour coffee in a tin cup. He handed me the cup of coffee,
an empty pie tin, and a folding spoon. I helped myself to
some of the dried-out looking beans and two biscuits. The
food was still warm. He watched me while I ate and sipped
on the black coffee. When I finished eating, I walked over
and poured water on the plate and cup to clean them up a
little bit and set them on the wagon seat.

"That was warming. Many thanks for your hospitality,"
I said as I came back and squatted down near the fire.

Feeling tired from all the turmoil of the day, I rolled me
a smoke and commenced to watch Stinson. It looked to me
like he was acting nervous about something. About every
other minute he would stop and look down the road beyond
the fire. He didn't have much of anything to say either.

"The young woman in miner's pants over at Blake's office told me you wanted to sell your claim," I said, hoping
to get some conversation started.

"That there's Captain Blake's wife's daughter, so I understand." He said, spitting tobacco. "She's only about
eighteen years old another miner told me, but Blake leaves
her to run that office by herself most of the time."

Stinson kept on talking. It seemed to me like he sounded
more than a little nervous. "I've heard it said that Blake's
got a mine of his own in some hidden place he found way
up in those rocks behind the cabin."

I thought about that for a minute. That young woman is
Blake's stepdaughter. Well of all things. I wondered if she
knew anything about Jim's disappearance. Or even if she
knew how Blake got ahold of Shell Mountain. My mind
had gotten set on the idea that Blake was behind Jim's
kidnapping. It seemed like the only reasonable thing to believe. I hated to think of that young woman being mixed
up in such a mess.

After thinking that through a time or two, I figured to
myself that even if she knew everything that was going on
she couldn't do anything to stop it. Not even if she wanted

to. She'd be obliged to do what her stepfather said for her to do.

Anxious to get back to my business I looked over at Stinson and asked, "How much of a claim have you got here?"

Stinson stood up. "I brought one square as Captain Blake calls the claims he sells. What it works out to be is just over an acre of ground. My piece runs a little more than a hundred feet alongside this road here and then it's about three hundred feet deep, give or take a tad. We're sitting on one outside edge of it." He pointed toward the lake and then back up the road. "I ain't been here long myself, only a little more than a month." Stinson continued. "The claims were all sold out when I got to the mine office, so I bought this claim off the digger that got it from Blake. He'd done got what gold he came here for. He got his stake right quick too, and he was ready to go home."

"That fella musta been some-kind of lucky. Somebody told me that this place ain't been open much more than a month." I said.

"That's right. And he was a lucky man about the gold, that's a fact. He told me when I bought the claim offen him that he hit a pocket of nuggets while he was cleaning out the spring that's up on the hill there, right near the opening to the tipple. He said he got more out of that one little hole in a few minutes than he got in two weeks of work on the shaft."

What Stinson described as his mining claim wasn't more than a shirt-tail of land to a cattleman, but I knew I had a lot to learn about mining. I got to my feet then and looked around the camp. We were sitting about a hundred feet from the edge of the lake. The land sloped kinda gentle like down to the edge of the water, but it started to go up sharply just beyond where the wagon was sitting. I couldn't spot the opening of a shaft from where I was standing. I figured it was up near the top of the bank.

"Have you found any color?"

Stinson tipped his head back down so the hat shaded his face again.

"I found enough."

"Why are you selling your claim out so quickly? I know for a fact you haven't been here but a few weeks."

I just asked him plain. I've always figured the only way to talk about money is flat out.

"They's been three men killed by bushwhackers in the last ten days or so. And worse than that, four or five others I know of outright disappeared from the diggings. Whoever it is that jumps these men catches them on the road to Belden when they're leaving outa here. They go out of our sight, but they never reach Belden or any place else. One of the men that was killed on the road was the fella I bought this here claim from. He didn't make it no more than a mile down the mountain before some sidewinders shot him down like you would a suck-egg coyote. They took all his stuff and stripped him. Some strangers found his naked body lying alongside the road."

Stinson was pacing up and down as he talked. "I got me a sick wife and two little boys waiting for me up to Colorado Springs. I ain't no good to them dead."

He looked up again when he said that. His eyes bored into mine, and he looked sort of scared, but determined. I studied his face for a second, and decided he looked to be talking straight.

"What kinda money are you wanting to turn loose of your claim?"

He just sat there and stared at me for a minute, then he spoke in what I thought was sort of a taunting voice.

"You ain't afraid of getting jumped?"

"Sure I am," I answered, staring right back at him. "I'm as scared as the next man, but I'm a fair hand with a gun and you've warned me. I can usually handle trouble if I know it's coming."

Stinson began to look a little bit more hopeful after I said that. He stopped pacing up and down and came back over to squat down by the fire.

"I give three hundred for the claim," he said eagerly. "I'd take that and throw in all the tools and improvements to boot."

"Well, I think I'll more than likely take that deal, but I'd be obliged if I could have a chance to look things over a little more first."

"Well of course, of course,"

Stinson was brightening up considerable. "I expected you'd want to look over the ground and the equipment and everything. It's a good claim. You'll see that right away. You're welcome to camp up here with me tonight if you want. I'll show you over everything tomorrow morning soon's its light. I allow we'll both be safer moving around out in the open when its daylight anyhow."

Saying my thanks for supper and all, I jumped up on the seat of the buckboard to move it around so I could park it close by Stinson's wagon. After I got the grays unhitched I put hobbles on them. There was only a little grass growing here and there for them to nibble on and I was afraid they would wander looking for more. I had planned for scarce feed though, and packed me a generous bag of oats in the buckboard. I could give them a good feed in the morning. They were used to having grain everyday.

I finished fooling with the horses and unrolled my bedroll on what looked like soft ground over near the buckboard. Stinson yelled goodnight. I looked up to see him disappearing into his wagon.

I woke up early the next morning and walked down to the edge of Shell Lake just about time the sun came up. Daylight showed the awful damage that a mining camp can work on what was once about the prettiest place in these mountains.

The whole area, all around the lake as far as you could

see, was dotted with miner's tents, wagons, rough-looking, tumbledown shacks, and piles of tree limbs and other trash. Patches of raw dirt showed up everywhere. It was hard for me to believe this was the same peaceful place I left last fall. I knew Jim would mortally hate what had been done to it.

When I came back up from the lake with a bucket of fresh water, Stinson was climbing over the tailgate of his wagon. He was still holding his rifle.

"Morning," he muttered as he walked over to squat down and punch up the fire he had banked the night before. He fussed with the fire a few minutes. When he was finally satisfied with it, he walked over to the back of the wagon and filled the coffeepot with water.

Without the miner's hat hanging down over his eyes I could see that Stinson was a heck of a lot younger than I'd taken him for the night before. It still seemed like I could see a scared look about him though. He was probably just a storekeeper or some kind of town worker who decided he'd take a flyer at mining, hoping to make enough to get himself set up somewhere.

He really looked a lot like an ordinary old dirt farmer though, but he claimed to be from Colorado Springs. There sure ain't many farms to be had in that town.

I helped Stinson rustle us up some breakfast, and wash up after we finished. He worked quickly, and still didn't have much to say. I offered him a smoke with his coffee, but he shook his head, holding up a twist of home-cured. When we finished putting things to rights he got his hat on and motioned for me to follow as he led the way up the hill to his diggings.

As soon as we walked around the big wagon, the opening of his little shaft was clearly visible in the bright sunlight. From this distance the adit looked about the size of a badger's hole. It was set almost all the way up to the top of the hill.

The slope of the land was sharp. I'd guess the angle wasn't a whole lot less than going straight up. We were both almost climbing on all fours by the time we reached the ledge in front of the shaft opening.

Stinson, or the fella who owned the claim before he did, had built himself a sort of platform out of dirt and rocks at the front of the opening of the shaft. It made a level place that was a good fifteen feet wide. That probably made working the rock a whole lot easier.

It looked to me like the dirt and gravel they used to build the platform must have come out of the mineshaft. The flat place narrowed down until it weren't much more than about three feet wide and that part extended off to the left for close to thirty feet. It ended up in some bushes near a couple of small stunted looking cottonwood trees.

Either Stinson or the other miner had set up a small sluice box on that level place to help him work the gold out of the waste rock and dirt. The contraption had a trough coming in to it made out of two boards fitted together so they looked like a vee from one end. The trough was propped up on spindly-looking posts that ran alongside the narrow path all the way up to the spring.

From where I was standing, I could see that the end piece of the trough, the one closest to the spring, was propped up higher than the spring. It seemed to be resting on top of a wooden door or gate. Stinson had rigged the trough so when he wanted water to run down to the sluice all he had to do was remove that prop to let the end of the trough down level with the spring and open a gate to let the water flow through.

Best I could tell from just looking, the rig was fixed so the runoff water from the sluice flowed through another one of those plank troughs until it got to where it was past the edge of the platform. Then it could run on down the hill and out of the way. If the outfit worked like I figured it

would, it was a real cute trick that would save a whole lot
of back-breaking work.

Watching and listening carefully as Stinson talked, I tried
not to let on how completely ignorant I was about mining.
I walked over to look inside the adit. The end of a long,
narrow stone boat was visible, sitting a little way back in
the shaft. It had a rope tied on to one end for pulling a
load.

There was a pick, a shovel, and a sledgehammer lying
on top on the sled. I reckoned that's what Stinson used to
haul dirt and rocks out to the sluice after he got them dug
out of the mountainside. He probably broke the stuff up
with the sledgehammer. I don't know much about mining,
and I hate the thought of a sledgehammer, but I surely
know what to do with a shovel and pick. They're what
cattlemen use for building fences, the worst job in ranching.

"Did you rig up this water trough?" I asked.

"Jackson, the man I bought the mine from, thought it out
and built it himself. The runoff water normally goes down
to the lake right along where those weeds are." Stinson
pointed to some low bushes and two crooked trees growing
at the end of the narrow ledge that led up hill from the dirt
platform. A trickle of water was running down the hill
away from it. "Only thing I have to do is climb up there
and set the trough in place where that wooden gate is. I get
a good enough flow of water to work my sluice."

"Blake couldn't have known anything about that spring
being there when he sold this claim to Jackson. He'd a
surely wanted two prices for the claim had he known there
was good water on it. He mightn't a even sold it at all."

Stinson was surely right about that. I nodded in agreement. If Blake had known about the spring he would never
have sold that claim. I sure wouldn't have. About that time
I noticed two big wooden buckets attached to a shoulder
yoke sitting on the ground close behind the sluice box.

Bless Pat, I thought to myself. *Doggoned if that rig don't look too much like work for my comfort.* It gave me a twinge between my shoulder blades to even look at the thing. I was almighty thankful I wouldn't have to use that rig to haul enough water to work a sluice.

Keeping quiet to hide my ignorance, I kept listening while Stinson went ahead on explaining the workings of his equipment. I nodded now and again, trying to look like I was really understanding everything he was telling me. Mining ain't no fine art, I surely know that much, and I figure I ought to be able to make a respectable show of it without too much of a problem.

Stinson finally turned and led the way inside the hole in the hill. We both had to stoop way over to keep from knocking our hats off. After we got a little way along in the shaft, I could see where he had set some beams across the roof with uprights at each end. They were cobbled together to look something like the framing of a door. I took it for granted they were holding up the dirt and rocks over top of our heads and was downright thankful to see them standing there.

Pretty soon Stinson stopped beside a pile of lumber that turned out to be a couple of dozen more of those sawed beams exactly like the ones rigged up over our heads. They were stacked along one side of the shaft.

"The fella I bought the mine from hauled in these here oak beams," Stinson commented. "They ain't easy to come by up here. I been mighty thankful I was able to buy them from him when I took over the mine. I put up the frame over where I been working no more than two days ago, so you won't need to use no more of these until you get a few feet deeper. The overhead here's awful soft, though. You're better off to put up a frame like these here about every two feet to keep yourself safe. When you work in a hole like this by yourself, you got to be forehanded or you could end up dead real easy."

I wasn't feeling one bit comfortable with that rock over-top of me, so I just sort of mumbled my answer. I was breathing kind of shallow by that time and sincerely hoping he didn't expect us to stay in this hole much longer. It felt to me like the roof was moving closer to my head every single minute.

Stinson picked up a lantern that was sitting on top of the stack of beams and struck a match to light it. He held it up high to get as much light out of it as he could and kept walking deeper into the hill. It was only a few more steps to where you could see the place he'd been working. When he held the light just right I could see a narrow seam of rotten quartz running across the end of the shaft. It was kind of a motley-gray color mingled with streaks of purple.

"Right here's where I've been finding my best color. There ain't no jewelry rock, mind you, but if you'll bend your back, this here kind of rock will pay you for working better than most. I hit this here seam of quartz about the second week after I got the claim, and as I told you last night, I'm ready to go home and tend to my family. I've got enough for a good stake." Stinson swung the lantern around so he could see my face.

It was easy to see that he really wanted me to buy the mine. I knew that if I was really serious about dealing for this claim I'd be trying to dicker with Stinson to get his asking price down some. I didn't think that would be hard to do either. He was showing his need to sell way too much. I could probably get the mine and equipment for a whole lot less than he was asking.

Saying a little prayer to myself that Stinson would be so anxious to sell that he wouldn't notice how anxious I was to buy, I decided there was just no time for me to be playing games about it.

"I'll take it," I said. "It looks good to me."

"Mining's hard, dirty work," Stinson said, "but you can take a few grains of gold a day, working like this.

"If there's any real serious pay dirt up here," he continued, "It's deep down inside the mountain, and knowing Colorado, it's probably gonna be silver instead of gold. I figure it's going to take a lot of money for anybody to make much more than good wages in these diggings. The gold I've been finding is mixed in with that vein of rotten quartz, so it's been easy to separate and work. There's no way to know how long that will last. I can't guarantee you it won't run out tomorrow. If you know anything at all about mining, you got to know that."

Walking around some, I studied the sluice for a few minutes and tried to take in everything. The claim was exactly what I had in mind. It would give me a good reason to be up here and I'd have a chance to try to find out Jim's whereabouts without anybody suspecting I was anything other than a miner. I kept hoping I might even be able to puzzle out a way to get the best of those crooks and get Jim his ranch back.

If he's still alive, that is—there seemed to be no way to keep myself from thinking that awful thought every once in a while.

Shaking my head to get back to the present, I told Stinson again, "I'm satisfied with what I see. I'll take the mine at your price."

Then I added. "I'm pretty strong. Maybe I can make it pay enough to be a worthwhile thing for me to do."

"Well, you should be able to make your money back quick enough," he answered. I could tell by his expression that he was relieved and pleased at my decision to take the mine off his hands. I reached out to shake on the deal.

Stinson was almost babbling as he said, "Thank you, Mr. Kendrick. Thank you. I'm obliged to you."

We slipped and slid back down to the wagon and got our business done. When I paid Stinson he almost grabbed the three hundred dollars right out of my hand. When he was ready to go he came over to me and offered to shake hands again.

"Use what you can of the junk I'm leaving, Kendrick. I've got to shake my stumps to get down the road toward Belden before nightfall. I ain't looking to end up lying dead in the road like the man I bought this mine from did."

He didn't even take his wagon with him when he left. He just packed up some of his stuff, loaded it on one of his mules, and rode the other one bareback. He was gone out of there before the sun was high.

It kind of flabbergasted me that the man would just ride off and leave his wagon. That surely took care of one of my questions. Stinson plainly was no farmer. Even a sick wife would hardly make a real farmer abandon his wagon. I couldn't help but notice that the closer he got to being ready to leave Stinson acted more and more like he was seriously scared he would run into trouble on the way down the mountain.

I couldn't help worrying a little myself as I watched him ride out of sight around the curve of the road. He had to have some gold he'd taken out of the mine, and I knew he had the three hundred dollars I just paid him for the claim. Considering what he said about miners being killed and robbed and disappearing, it was plainly dangerous for him to be leaving this place alone.

Chapter Four

Lt took me the rest of the morning to get myself settled in. My tent was a good-sized one and I had me a folding cot so I wouldn't have to sleep on the ground. I hated that. No matter how much grass there is or how carefully a body cleans up the rocks and sticks, the doggoned ground is just plain hard.

I guess hating to sleep on the ground comes from working cattle since I was a kid. I spent many a night in a bedroll lying on the dirt. I had planned on never doing it again. I guess I could hope last night would be the last time.

After I got my tent set up right and all my stuff situated so I could be comfortable, I stowed all my supplies away under the cot in the tent. Then I went over and took a stick of wood to chunk the fire up real good and set a fresh pot of coffee to boil. When it was ready it went down real smooth with two of those big sandwiches and a piece of apple pie Miss Hetty packed in that little basket she put in the buckboard.

About the time I finished eating my dinner I looked up for some reason. I could see a figure walking toward me around the lake. It was a man coming from the same direction Stinson had taken when he left—from somewhere back toward the mine office and the road to town.

The man was still pretty far away when I first noticed him, but even from that distance I could tell he was moving like he was sick or something was wrong with him. Then the thought occurred to me that maybe he was drunk. He was walking along sort of careful like, taking kinda short steps, and now and again he would stagger a little bit like he'd made a misstep.

As he got up closer so I could see him a little better, something about the way the fella held himself made me think he was nothing but a boy. I made sure my colt was ready just in case and walked over beside the tent. I reached down and dropped the flap over the opening to kinda hide my belongings some. Then I moved back near the fire to watch him approach.

As soon as he got close enough so I could see his face good and clear, it was plain this was no grown man. He was nothing but a young kid. He had the height of a grown man, and considerably more than some, but now that I could see his face good he looked like he was no more than twelve or thirteen years old.

His hair was black or a real dark brown and curled tight to his head. I figured that if he was any older than thirteen he would surely have a little bit of hair on his face. There'd be some fuzz on his upper lip at least.

I straightened up as the boy approached the camp and hailed him.

"Hello there."

He didn't answer me, so I said, "Come on over here to the fire, son. I've still got a little coffee in the pot and there's a couple of sandwiches left over from my lunch if you're hungry."

The boy came up close to the fire. He stood right straight across from me for about a second then folded up his long legs to sit down on the ground. When he raised his head to look up at me again I could see tears on his cheeks.

His voice sounded kind of choked as he said, "I spoke to Mr. Stinson up the road a ways. He said you might be needing some help working your claim, Mr. Kendrick. I know what to do on a claim and I'm a hard worker."

I felt sort of shocked when I saw the tears running down the boy's face, and I couldn't help but wonder how much work a kid could do when he was so weak that he couldn't walk straight, but I didn't say anything about that. I went over to the tent and got Aunt Hetty's basket with what was left of the sandwiches and pie. I didn't have but one cup, so I rinsed it out and poured him some coffee.

The boy's hands were shaking when he reached up and took the sandwiches from me. He unwound the napkin off one sandwich and took a small bite, chewing that first mouthful for a long time. It came to me all of a sudden that he might be shaky from not eating. He was sure nibbling at that sandwich like somebody who'd been so starved he couldn't hardly handle food when he finally got some.

There didn't seem to be anything to say. I watched the boy eat for a few minutes then I went over to see what was left inside the yellow-topped wagon Stinson had abandoned. There looked to be little more than some old clothes lying scattered around on the floor of the wagon bed. There were several blankets piled on a bunk that was built in along one side.

When I pulled my head out from under the wagon cover and stepped back down to the ground, I noticed a box with a lid attached to the outside of the wagon. I walked around and opened it to find a tin plate, a cup, and a frying pan, with a few other things necessary for cooking and eating. Stinson had left more than I thought.

If that boy was serious about wanting work, I had me an

idea. I left the wagon and went back to my spot across the fire from the kid. He had finished eating one of the sandwiches and was working his way through the second.

"I reckon if Stinson recommended you I'll give you a try. I could sure use your help. I couldn't pay you regular wages, but I'll give you a share of what we dig out of that hole up on the hill."

Watching the boy's face, it seemed to me like he was looking a little bit less done in. Either he had been dog-tired enough to about fall over when he walked into camp or he really had been about to faint from being hungry. I guess it could have been some of both.

He looked like he might be about the age when young boys get so they can eat enough grub to founder two or three grown men. He kept on eating that sandwich, but he was looking at me so hard and sort of scared like, that I was almost starting to feel a little bit guilty. I don't know what it was I was supposed to feel guilty for doing, but that's the way I was feeling.

When he finally finished eating the sandwich and took another sip of the coffee, the boy sighed and sort of smiled.

"I'd be obliged to work your mine for my keep and a share of what we find, Mr. Kendrick. I've been on my own for a while now and meals haven't been coming too regular lately."

"It looked a little bit like you were sick or drunk when you first came around the bend there. Do you mind telling me how it happens you're out here on your own? You look a mite young not to have somebody looking out for you."

"My Pa and I were working a claim over beyond that first hill up behind the mine office. We were one of the first ones to buy a claim up here. We dug us a shaft and had finally started finding a little color. We were actually getting a few grains of gold almost every day. It was never very much at all, but Pa said it paid better than wages.

"Pa was kneeling down by the fire making our supper

one night. It was just about dusky-dark. I had gone to a spring that's right close by there to get us a bucket of fresh water for drinking with our supper and making coffee the next morning. While I was down at the spring I heard two or three horses running. Then I heard shots fired up at our camp. I had enough sense to run back into the little patch of woods near the spring and hide in some bushes.

"After I got over being so scared, I crept up near enough to our claim to see what had happened. Pa was lying face down in the dirt near our tent. I think he must have been trying to get to his shotgun when they shot him. One of the claim jumpers had turned his pockets inside out. I knew right off that he was dead.

"Three men were sitting around the campfire eating our supper like nothing had even happened. I almost made a noise about then I felt so bad, but Pa had taught me to be careful around strangers. It seemed clear to me that if those men knew I existed they would chase me down and kill me too."

"Did you know any of the men who bushwhacked your father?"

I was suddenly full up with questions. I wondered to myself if those claim jumpers could have been Blake's men?

Could it be possible that a gang of outlaws was running the whole mining operation? Could they be the same men who kidnapped Jim and left the note demanding money from the Major?

"I know who the three men are who killed my Pa." The boy said softly, "they don't know I saw their faces, but I know them. I'll always know them."

That kid's voice sounded really cold when he said that. It was plain to me that the boy was planning to find a way to punish the men that killed his father. Looking at the expression on his face I had to think he just might do it one of these days.

"What did you do then?"

"I worked my way through the woods and over near the lake where I couldn't be seen from the camp. Then I walked a mile or more higher up on the mountain and hid in a clump of bushes. I stayed up there until the next day, and then I came back down close to our place to see what was going on. I crept up quiet like through the woods to where I could see our campsite. One of the men was working our diggings just like they were his own. Pa's body was gone.

"I noticed a spot where it looked like some dirt had been freshly turned over. It was on the pile of waste Pa and me had hauled out of our tipple. I guessed that was Pa's grave."

"Couldn't you go to Blake for help?

"No. I knew two of those men sitting by the campfire had been hanging around Blake's office. They were probably working for him all the time."

I caught my breath when he said that. It fitted with what I was thinking.

"Well, I sat there and watched the men for a while, and then it came to me that the best thing I could do was make a way to live for myself. I knew I was going to have to have some help. All I had to my name was the clothes I was standing up in and the wooden bucket I had taken to the spring that night. I didn't even have a heavy coat to wear or a blanket to sleep in, besides having no gun to hunt game and no money to buy supplies. I was hungry then, and had already almost frozen that one night I spent in the woods. It had rained for hours that night and I got soaked."

"Don't you have some family somewhere you could go back to?"

"No, Sir. There was no one but Pa and me. My Ma died when I was a baby. I never knew her. If we had any other folks I don't remember ever seeing them or even hearing Pa talk about them. Pa was a mover. He was an educated man, but he couldn't stay long in one place.

"I can remember several different times we stopped in a town and he worked as a blacksmith and gunsmith for the winter months, but we were always strangers when we got to a town and still strangers when we left it. We didn't ever stay more than a year in any one place. If I've got other family somewhere, I sure don't know where they are."

"I'm sorry about your father, son. That's a rough break for a youngster. Go ahead and tell me what you did after you left the claim."

"Pa had been sort of friendly with another miner by the name of Sherman Deal. He works a claim over east of where Pa and me were located. He would come over to our camp sometimes at night and he and Pa would play cards together. He always acted real kindly toward me."

"I went over to Deal's place and told him how Pa was killed by the claim jumpers and asked if he would hire me to help him work his claim. He said he would be right glad to have me work for my keep, but he hadn't found any color yet so he couldn't agree to pay me wages.

"Working with Deal went fine there for a while. He always spoke to me kindly, and he fed me good. He even gave me this old blanket coat to wear. But one day he left the dig early. When I went to the camp I noticed he had found a bottle somewhere, or maybe he had it all along, I don't know."

"He sent me to get water, and when I brought it back I jarred the bucket when I went to sit it down and spilled a little. Deal swung at me with a chunk of wood and called me a bad name. I took off running with him chasing me. He was yelling and cussing and threatening what all he was going to do to me when he caught me."

The boy stopped talking and looked up at me with haunted eyes. His cheeks had turned kinda reddish and he looked like he was about to bust out crying. He managed to start talking again.

"I've been living wild ever since. I caught some rabbits

in my snares now and again, and found some pine nuts to eat, but I couldn't find near enough to fill up on. What with the mining and so many people living around here, most of the small animals have been scared away. The digging destroyed a lot of the natural things a body could usually find to eat too."

I was feeling mighty sorry for that boy by the time he finished talking.

"Forget all that, son, you did right to run away. You can have that wagon over there for your place. It ain't all that much, but at least you'll be out of all this infernal rain. I've got my tent, and I promise you'll never have to be afraid of me getting drunk or cussing you either."

I stood up and kept on talking,

"Most people call me Ken. You haven't told me your name."

The boy straightened up to his full height and held out his hand to shake mine, "I'm William Tell Davis. My Pa always called me Will."

I knew it wasn't too polite in me and the boy might resent me for it, but I couldn't help but ask, "How old are you Will?"

Will looked a little bit exasperated, but he answered me politely, "I'll be fourteen the first day of November, Sir."

"You look a little younger than that to me, but you should grow out to be a fair sized man, if you're only thirteen."

"My Pa measured right at six feet tall without his boots and I'm already near as tall as he was. I doubt if I'll top you though Mr. Kendrick."

"Look here, Will. I appreciate manners in a youngster, but you're almost a man growed and living on your own. You call me Ken."

"Thank you, Sir. I'll do that."

The boy's face looked more relaxed, as though he was beginning to feel a little more comfortable about me.

"I'll tell you what, Will."

It come to me that the boy should probably take things kinda slow until he got another meal or two under his belt. I was fairly sure he wouldn't want me to say any such thing, so I sort of talked around it.

"Doggoned if the morning ain't plumb gone. I hate to start a job in the middle of the day, so let's take the rest of the day to get all our gear in good shape. I better clean and oil my guns and tend to my team, and you could help get us some wood and water in case we have some more bad weather. I haven't even took time yet to look over the tools up at the mine. I don't know if Stinson kept them sharp and oiled or not. We'd better go over them to make sure, don't you think? We can get everything ready and then start in seriously working at this mining business tomorrow morning."

"There's plenty of firewood we could get up by the eastern side of the lake if you've got an axe." The boy seemed eager to work. I guess he wanted to show me he'd be worth his salt.

Well now Wayne Kendrick, I thought, almost laughing at myself. *What he probably wants to show me is that he'll be worth his meals.*

"There's an axe in that tool box on the back of the buckboard. We'll use that to chop up some deadfalls. There's a little stone boat up at the mine too. We can use it to haul the wood back to camp on.

"You go get the inside of the wagon straightened out to suit you first, Will. I'll sit here and get busy on my guns. When we get that all done, we'll both go fetch us some wood."

After I watched the boy climb into the wagon, I went over and pulled a bag of speckled beans out of my supplies. I rinsed out the coffeepot and poured in what looked to me like about a pound of the beans and covered them with water so they could soak. I settled the pot in the coals of the fire so the beans would simmer and be ready to cook for our supper.

It was plain to me that if we were gonna have enough to eat I would have to make a trip up on the mountain and shoot us a deer or an elk some day soon. I could eat something most any time a day my own self. I had made certain to lay in plenty of food supplies to last me for several days, but it would be a easy thing for a growing boy the size of Will to burn up enough fixins for two men.

My head was almost spinning. I was thinking a mile a minute, and felt like jumping up and down I was so impatient. I was going to let the boy settle down some now, but before dark I intended to find out what he knew about this Blake operation, and if he had seen anything when he was "living wild" that might help me find Jim.

My money said he had.

By suppertime my head was aching with all the questions I wanted to ask Will Davis. We had packed in a pile of broken up deadfall on the little stone boat, pulled it back down to camp, and piled it under the wagon so we'd have some dry wood in case it kept on raining.

In between trips to get wood, I had chunked up the fire and set the beans and a can of tomatoes to cooking in a big spider. When the beans were done I poured us both a cup of coffee, sliced up some bread I had bought from Mrs. Southwood and dished up our food. We settled over near the fire to eat.

Will dug in to those beans like a starving wolf, exactly the way I figured he would, but I found that I was so strung out from worrying my appetite was gone.

I looked down at my plate of beans and studied on things for a little while longer, then I finally faced it. There was nothing else for it. I had to trust the boy.

"Will, I came up here for a purpose other than mining gold." I said.

The boy looked at me sort of slant-ways when I said that.

"A good friend of mine used to live up on the mountain here in that very cabin that Blake calls his mining office. He had filed on this whole area and was starting him a ranch. I came up here and helped him do the work the government requires to prove up on his claim late last summer."

"How did Blake get the ranch then?"

"I don't rightly know that."

"Did your friend sell the claim to Blake?"

"I know he didn't sell his ranch to Blake," I said heatedly. "He just wouldn't have done that. Making himself a ranch on this mountain was like a dream come true for Jim Cason.

"My ranch is out a good distance and I don't get into town all that often, so I only found out about the gold mining and Blake taking over up here a little before noon yesterday. It was a terrible shock to me, I'll tell you that.

"At first I just knew my friend Jim was dead. It was the only thing that figured. I knew he would never give up his dreams peaceable. I was sure Blake would've needed to kill him to get him out of here.

"Well, I made tracks out to Jim's home to tell his father what was happening. When I got there Major Cason tried to keep it a secret by lying to me, but I found out from Jim's sister that somebody had come to their house and stuck a ransom note under the front door.

"It's just a couple of days ago that it happened. The note demanded that the Major pay whoever it was that wrote it ten thousand dollars. It said that if the Major didn't pay the money they would kill Jim.

"It seemed clear to me right then that I had to try to do something to find Jim, so I lit on the idea of coming up here and pretending to be a miner. I figured I could find out what's going on and maybe get a lead on where the kidnapper's are holding Jim without anybody noticing me."

I watched the boy as he studied me. I had me a notion that he might save Jim's life if he knew something.

Then he completely astonished me by saying, "I've seen a place up on the mountain where men are kept chained up."

"What? Men are kept chained up? Explain what you mean by that." I demanded. I was shaking inside.

"I saw a bunch of men working at a mine. Every one of them wore chains on their arms and legs. The place where I saw 'em is way up on that higher mountain, over behind the mining company's cabin. I think its Captain Blake's mine. I guess it's possible your friend could be one of those men."

"Tell me what you saw."

"I found the place when I was out hunting one day. I hadn't seen a sign of a deer close by here, so I went up higher on that next mountain than I usually did. It must have been about the first week of March.

"Something was making a banging noise. It sounded like a sledgehammer hitting on rock to me, so I climbed up on a sort of rocky hill or wall and looked over the top in the direction of the noise. I could see down into a sort of box canyon where some men were working in a bunch of boulders. The opening of a mine was right behind them. There were eight men that I could count from where I was.

"The men were too far away for me to see all of them clearly, but the ones I got a good look at had chains on their wrists and ankles. One man was standing guard over them. He was walking up and down and holding a Greener across his arm."

"What did you do?"

"Well, the first thing I did was get the heck out of there without daring to make a sound. The whole thing looked plumb scary to me.

"The sight of those poor men gave me such a bad feeling that I gave up on the idea of hunting that day and walked on back down to our camp. When I got back there and told Pa what I had seen he acted like he was almost mad with me for even finding the place.

"Pa ordered me to keep my mouth shut and stay well away from the mountaintop. Later on, I guess he sort of calmed himself down some, because he apologized for getting so excited. He told me he thought the men I saw with the chains on their arms and legs were likely a bunch of county convicts Captain Blake brought up here to work his gold mine."

"Could you go back to this place, Will? Could you guide me up there?"

I was so excited my heart was thumping. It felt like it was gonna jump out of my chest. Tom Dillard heard about men disappearing from up here, and Stinson was complaining about men disappearing out of the camp. It occurred to me that there was a possibility that the men wearing chains were the same ones that had disappeared.

"Are you thinking that your friend could be one of those chained-up men Captain Blake has got working his mine?" The boy's eyes went wide when he realized his supposition was exactly right.

"He might be, Will. I hate to think of such a thing, but it's certainly possible. I know I've surely got to go up there and find out if he is or not."

"I can go back to the place easily enough," Will nodded his curly head, with a look of complete confidence. "It's a far piece up through the woods though, even with no snow on the ground. As I remember, it took me several hours to climb up there on foot."

"I've got the horses we can use. I don't have saddles, though. You can ride bareback can't you?"

Will shot me a sort of half-irritated look and answered in a dry voice.

"Yes, Mr. Kendrick, I can ride a horse bareback."

I had to chuckle at that.

"Sorry Will. I reckon I better remember what I said about you being a man growed."

It was just after dark when Will and me left camp. He led the way as we rode to the east and uphill around the lake. He said it was the best way to go to make sure none of the miners or any of Blake's men noticed us starting out that time of day.

Aunt Hetty's grays were as calm as you could ever want horses to be. They seemed to be undisturbed by the indignity of being ridden with only a rope hackamore. I noticed that Will certainly handled the horse without a problem.

The possibility of finding Jim had me so excited that I wanted to run the horses to get there as fast as we possibly could, but we kept to a walk. Some nosy person would be sure to wonder what in the world was going on if they heard our horses running along the lake after dark.

I was dressed for working my way up near the mine as soon as we got close. I had changed my boots for moccasins, figuring I could get around a lot quieter like that, and I was carrying my rifle across my lap.

It took us nearly an hour to get around the lake. About that time we came up on a heavy stretch of pine trees. As soon as we rode about a hundred yards alongside the trees, Will turned his horse sharply away from the lake and led us straight into the woods. He kept on going, holding a straight line for what I guessed was nearly a mile.

He finally turned his horse again to go up the hill, traveling as true as if he was following a road or railroad track. It took us a while. It was so dark in under the trees we couldn't move fast for fear of hurting the horses or half-killing ourselves by running into branches.

We walked the horses up the mountain. That part of the trip took us close to another hour. The woods finally began to thin out so we could see a little better, then we reached the tree line and rode out into the open. The moon had come up by that time, and it was bright enough so we could see a fair distance.

Clicking my tongue to my horse, I hurried him up a little so I could ride alongside Will and asked, "How much farther is it to this place?"

He thought a minute before he answered.

"It's only about another mile I'd say. It's almost directly ahead of us. We'll have to leave the horses soon, and walk the rest of the way up to the ridge. I remember a good place for them to stay. The rocks get too rough to risk the horses pretty soon now, and we don't want to take a chance on anybody at the mine hearing them."

"I want you to stay with the horses."

"I can't do that," Will's voice sounded overly quiet and logical.

I thought he sounded sort of like somebody talking to a little kid.

"The way that place is hidden you'll never find it unless I go along and show you where it is. Remember Ken, I only found the place myself by pure accident. I could describe it to you all day long, but you'd still not be able to find it."

"All right. I'll give you that, but you show me where the mine is and then I want you to get yourself back to where we leave the horses and wait for me."

I tried to sound stern and positive.

"Before I start out we'll try to figure how long it should take me to get near enough to that mine to find out something. Then we'll add some more time for me to get myself out of there and back down to where you're waiting."

I noticed that Will had turned his head and was looking away from me, but I continued on talking.

"If something happens to me I want you to take both of these horses and go straight down the mountain to Belden.

What I mean is—if I don't come back in the time we agree
it should take me, or if you hear shots fired up there, you're
to get out of here and try to get help."

I noticed again that Will kept looking away from me. It
felt kinda like he was ignoring me, but I kept on talking.

"Don't go near the road on the way, either. If you have
to go down the mountain, take your time and stay well-
hidden back in the pines until you're right near town. Ask
the first person you see to point out the way to Miss Hetty
Kendrick's house. Everybody knows her. If you don't see
anybody around to ask, turn one of the grays loose and just
follow him. Either one of them will lead you right to my
aunt's house.

"No matter what time you get there, you pound on her
door if you have to, just wake her up. Tell Miss Hetty
everything that's happened up here and she'll take it from
there. Is all that clear?"

"Are you saying that if something goes wrong up there
I should just run out on you?"

The boy stopped his horse and turned back around to
stare up in my face.

"Doggone it, kid," I felt an almost irrational rush of ag-
gravation and a sickening panicked feeling.

"That's not what I mean at all. You listen to me."

I was about to get myself upset. I stopped my horse
beside his and took the time to explain what I was thinking.

"This ain't no game we're playing, Will. If those miners
that disappeared around here are the one's Blake's got
chained up and working that mine for him, then this is dad-
blamed serious business. There's sure to be guards up there
like the one you saw with the prisoners. I could easily get
caught while I'm snooping around the place. If they do
catch me I want to know that you're free to go down to
Belden and get me some help. I ain't anxious to spend the
rest of my life in chains breaking rock for that Blake fella."

"Oh," Will said, acting as calm as you please. "That's different.

"Come on," he continued, talking over his shoulder as he nudged his horse to start it walking again. "We can ride a little bit farther. After we leave the horses I'll show you how to climb over the rocks where you can walk up nearer to the mine. After that I'll come on back down here and stay with the horses. I figure it will probably take you somewhere near thirty or forty minutes or maybe even a little longer to creep around and see everything up there."

Will led off up the mountain and my horse fell in behind his. I had to shake my head. I was beginning to wonder just who was the grown-up here. All of a sudden I wasn't feeling much like I was the one in charge of this expedition.

We made better time out in the bright moonlight. It wasn't but a few minutes before Will motioned with his left hand toward a small canyon. As we rode through the narrow opening I saw a trickle of water coming out of the rocks over to one side. It had formed a small pool. The ground was covered with thick grass. The little meadow was almost surrounded by great boulders that rose up higher than my head.

"We can leave the horses here and they'll be safe," Will said. "It's almost like a natural corral. There's plenty of grass and water, so they'll surely stay put."

I slid to the ground and fumbled at my belt for the two sets of soft hobbles I brought with me. With Will's help I got the ropes on the gray's front legs. While I was tying the hobbles, I got the impression that both the horses were a little insulted at me for putting the things on their legs.

The geldings are well trained and they're used to standing ground hitched, but they're Miss Hetty's animals, not mine. I wasn't about to take any chances on them wandering away just when we needed them the most.

Will and I began to climb. Rocks were scattered around on the ground. It looked as though some giants might have been throwing them at each other. We had to walk slowly so as not to make a noise by accidentally kicking one of those rocks into another. The going was treacherous. We were sure right to leave the horses and walk.

As we reached a sort of natural wall of jumbled rocks, Will turned around and motioned for me to wait. He used both hands to climb to the top of the wall. When he were almost there he put his finger up to his lips to warn me to be quiet, and raised his head to look over the edge. He studied the view beyond the rock for a few minutes then turned back and picked his way down the rocks to stand beside me.

"We're real close to the mine. I saw a man walking up and down in front of the largest cabin. I think he was holding a long gun of some sort. He must be guarding the miners."

"Let me get up there myself and take a look."

Pulling myself up on the rocks to the same place Will had been sitting, I looked over the edge. I immediately spotted the man near the cabin. He was walking in my direction. I could see what appeared to be the moonlight reflecting off a gun barrel. Will was right.

As I watched the man he turned his back to us and walked over to the other side of the cabin. He kept on walking around the corner and out of my sight. He was hidden from view for about a full minute, then came walking back where I could see him. I watched him repeat the pattern two more times. He was taking a little more then a full minute each time he walked back and forth.

I slid back down the little hill and whispered to Will.

"The guard stays out of sight a full minute or more every time he makes a pass. I think it gives me plenty of time to get over the crest and down into the shadows where I can't be seen. I'm going to try get closer. You go on back to the horses now, Will."

"How long do you think I should wait for you?"

"Give me at least two full hours. If you hear gun shots or yelling or I don't show up by that time, you hightail it out of here as fast as you can go. Remember what I said about staying away from the road and be careful. When you show up at Miss Hetty's house with those horses and tell her what's happening she'll stir up the whole countryside."

"Those men will kill you."

"I don't think so. Don't you worry none about me; I'm a pretty good Indian. With a little luck those fellas will never know I've been anywhere near their operation. I expect I'll be back with you well before two hours is past. Here, you take my rifle. I've got my hand gun and I think the rifle might get in my way."

Will stared hard at me for a blink or two. He had a serious look on his face, like he mighta been worried about me. He opened his mouth like he wanted to say something more, but apparently thought better of it. He finally turned away to walk downhill and disappear in the shadows.

Turning back to the wall, I crawled up to look over toward the mine buildings again. The guard was still pacing up and down in front of the largest cabin. He kept to a regular schedule. I counted the seconds as he went out of sight. After counting four more times I was certain the man was spending at least a full minute out of sight every time. I figured that if I made sure to be quick about it, he wouldn't have a chance to spot me when I crawled over the top of the rocks and down the other side.

There wasn't much to do to get myself ready. I took a couple of deep breaths to steady my nerves, and as soon as the guard turned to walk his beat again I rolled over the edge of the rocks and scrambled down to the level. Moving as quietly as I could, it seemed to take me forever to get in the shadows at the bottom of the wall where I couldn't be seen.

About the time I flattened myself out down behind some broken rocks, the guard came walking back around the corner of the cabin. I could see him perfectly from where I was hidden.

The man didn't change his pace or anything, so I felt assured he couldn't see me. I was certain he would yell or shoot or show some sort of reaction if he caught sight of me.

So far so good, I thought.

Keeping my head down, I waited where I was a few minutes. I needed time to get my breath back and calm down. My heart felt like it was going to pound a hole through my ribs. It almost seemed like it would be possible for the man over near the cabin to hear it beating. My hands were shaking.

Chapter Five

Finally, I began to crawl along in the shadows close to the edge of the rocks. It wasn't long until I came to some scattered aspens. It was dark enough in amongst the trees for me to stand up straight. I moved a few feet at a time and stood close to the tree trunks, hoping they would sort of blur my shape so I'd be hard to see if somebody happened to look directly at me.

In a few minutes I made it past a smaller cabin. I was still staying well back in the trees. I could hear the sound of voices coming from inside the building. They got a little louder as I got near the rear wall. I worked my way along close to the wall and turned the corner. From that angle I could see a small window high up on the side. I figured it would help me hear a little better.

One of the voices I'd been hearing was undoubtedly a woman's. It sounded high-pitched and light. I strained to hear what the people said, but they kept their voices so low it was impossible for me to make out any words.

After straining to hear the conversation for a few minutes, I heard footsteps crossing the wooden floor and the door of the cabin was flung open. I flattened myself

back against the side of the cabin so whoever was leaving
wouldn't be able to see me.

The door slammed shut and I heard the sound of metal
hitting metal. The clinking sounded to me like a lock being
fastened with a padlock. I kept still and listened, wondering
why the cabin would be locked.

Light footsteps headed away from the door and down the
hill. There was only one set of footsteps—only one person
was leaving. *The cabin was locked because there was a
prisoner inside.*

When the sound of footsteps got far enough away so I
felt a little safer, I sneaked a look around the front corner
of the cabin. I could see a small figure walking along toward the back of the big cabin where the guard was posted.
It occurred to me that the figure leaving this cabin was
more than likely that Blake woman I met up at the mine
office earlier.

The figure I was watching skirted around the big cabin
and walked across an open space to enter a third cabin that
was showing a light out of its open door. That cabin was
about twice as big as the one I was hiding behind.

Moving back to the far side of the cabin, I tried to look
in the little window but it was built too far up on the wall
for me to see inside without finding me something to climb
up on. I looked around for a rock or something like, but
couldn't find anything, so I finally gave it up and decided
to go see if I could find out anything useful by watching
that Blake woman.

Easing back into the trees a little ways, I started to walk
over closer to the other cabin. When I got near it, the light
was still shining out on the ground from the open door. I
worked myself into a position so I could see inside.

Sure enough, the same young woman I talked to down
in the mine office stood at a table in the middle of the room.
She was washing up some dishes and pans. I couldn't tell
for sure, but she didn't seem to be talking to anybody. It

appeared to me like she was alone in the cabin. At least I couldn't see or hear anybody else.

The woman stopped her work occasionally and stood with her hands in the dishpan to stare out of the open door. The expression on her face looked first sad and then angry. She seemed to be thinking hard about something. From where I was hiding I could see her face clearly by the light of the kerosene lamp that was sitting on the table beside the dishpan.

After I watched the woman for a minute or two I began to hear footsteps coming toward the cabin. They were coming from the general direction of the large cabin where I watched that guard walking up and down earlier. I hunkered down in the trees hoping that whoever it was coming wouldn't see me. No more'n a second later two men came out into view.

The men walked up to the cabin where the girl was working and stepped in the open door. They both stopped between the table and the door where I could get a good look at them. One stood right in the opening and leaned one shoulder up against the doorframe. He was just plain big. The tallest one of the men stepped over beside the table and commenced to yell at the woman.

"Ain't you finished cleanin' up this place from supper yet, girl? I swear, I think you get slower and lazier by the day."

"I had to feed the miners, Pa. There's eight of them out there now. Cooking for that many men and then cleaning up after it takes me some time." The girl went on working and held her head down as she answered.

"Don't you be sassing me, girl," the man said in a rough voice. "I been good to you. I got a right to expect you'd do what fixing around here you can do to help me. Them miners out there ain't much more than wild hogs. You got no call to take up so much time tending them."

"I've not been taking extra time for nothing, Pa. Don't

forget that one that's hurt. He's been having a bad time with his leg. I had to re-bind it for him again tonight. It wasn't healed enough for him to go in the mine to work. I told you that yesterday."

"I'll decide when a man's able to work. That one's been loafing around here too everlasting long anyway. He's just eating up food I pay good money for and taking up your time. He might not be up to a full day's work yet, but it don't take a whole lot of old Don here snapping his whip around to make him want to do all the work he's able. He might soon get to hate the whip enough for his leg to just miraculously heal up."

I decided right then that the man talking to the girl had to be that Captain Malcolm Blake. It was soon plain that the man he called Don was the heavy-set one that was leaning against the doorjamb. He laughed out loud when Blake mentioned that stuff about using a whip on the miners and stood up straight to reach over and slap the taller man on the back.

"The sight and sound of that old leather cat shore wakes them lazy bums up, don't it Mac," he said in a loud voice. He was still laughing as he leaned back against the doorway.

The tall man turned around to face the door. I couldn't see his features clear, the lamp was angled kind of behind him so the light didn't touch his face. He had to be Blake, though. He was almost as tall as me, but something about him made me decide he was considerably older. It was probably the way he moved that made me think that. His shoulders drooped a little, and I remembered noticing that he caught the doorjamb with one hand and sorta pulled himself up the step when he entered the cabin.

Blake's hair and beard were dark, but even from a distance I could tell it was full of silver streaks. I couldn't see his expression clear or tell the color of his eyes, but I was sure I would know him if I ever saw him again.

Blake leaned back against the edge of the table and rolled a smoke. After he fiddled with the tobacco and paper for a minute or two he raised his head and asked the other man, "Are you going to be ready early tomorrow night to ride down the mountain and tell that Cason boy's father where he should leave our money?"

"Do you really think that rancher can come up with ten thousand dollars, Captain?"

"I'd be willing to bet he had that money ready the same day we left the note. I'm also inclined to think we were simple fools when we asked for such a small amount of money. Ten thousand dollars is probably not much more than a drop in a bucket to that Major Cason."

"How do you figure that?"

"You saw his house when we took the note down there. His place is probably bigger than the governor's mansion."

"That's a fact."

The man called Mac crossed his arms and continued talking. "He'd better have that money ready and leave it exactly where I tell him to, or I'll make him a present of one of his boy's fingers every single day until he does pay up."

My heart started in to pounding again. I was so mad I wanted to take a gun and shoot both of the lowdown scheming devils right where they were standing.

It suddenly hit me that what the two men had just said meant that Jim was still alive. The relief I felt took every bit of starch out of my backbone. I was so weak right then I had to sit on the ground to keep from falling down.

When I looked back up toward the cabin the two men had moved away from the door. I could still hear them talking, but no matter how hard I tried I couldn't pick out the words. I figured they were planning out how they would go about getting their hands on the ransom money from the Major.

As I kept on watching, the young woman walked over to stand in the doorway. She tossed the water from the dishpan out onto the dirt path. Still holding the pan in both hands, she stood still for several minutes, staring out into the night. It felt eerily like she was staring right at me.

After a while she turned around and went back inside to sit the empty dishpan on the table, then she moved out of my sight. A few minutes later I heard her call goodnight to the two men.

There was no indication of where she was calling from, but I hoped to myself that her room had a thick door with a strong lock. Whether she was willingly helping Blake or not, it looked to me like she was in an awful place for a young woman.

I sat still and waited impatiently until one of the men came over and shut the door. The lamp went out a few minutes later. All was quiet in the cabin. The amount of time Will and I had agreed on me spending in the canyon was beginning to run low, but I had found out that Jim was alive. It occurred to me then that he might be that wounded man the girl talked about.

Easing my way around behind the cabin, I stood up straight and walked across the open area near the larger building, walking as quietly as I could. I wanted to see how many prisoners they had locked up in there. When I got in the shadow of the cabin, I was near the back corner of the building, diagonally opposite the corner where the guard walked.

Looking and feeling along the wall, I soon found one of the narrow cracks left where the chinking had fallen out from between the logs. The slit was angled so I could see inside. The moon was shining in a window on the other side of the cabin. I could see well enough to count eight men inside. They were sleeping on a platform nailed up against the far wall.

The platform-bed-thing looked sort of like a table with sides sticking up all the way round it. There was enough light for me to see that those sorry skunks had a log chain run from one end of the platform to the other. The chain was woven between the prisoner's ankles, above their shackles, and was attached to a ring in the logs at each end of the building.

My stomach lurched. *What kind of people could do such a thing?*

It was clear to me that if Jim was one of those poor devils I would surely have to find a way to get him out of there in the daytime. I might cut one of them ankle chains in two with a hatchet or axe blade—they looked to be pretty light—but I would never be able to break or cut that heavy log chain.

I decided I had seen more than enough for one night.

Turning back the way I came, I worked my way around to the rocks again as fast as I could, what with having to keep quiet and all. I didn't want to overstay the two hours. I wanted to get back down to camp and do some planning on how to approach this thing so I could get Jim out of here.

My climb back out of the canyon was easy enough. I chose a place to go up that was about forty feet to the west of where I rolled down off the bunch of rocks. There were more bushes and vines growing in that place to give me handholds, and I was hoping all the foliage would hide any marks my boots made on the face of the rocks. I figured it would at least blur my footprints enough so if anybody happened to look over there during the day they wouldn't notice anything.

When I came down on the other side of that little hill I practically ran across the rocks to where Will was waiting with the horses. I couldn't find him when I first entered the little meadow, but after about a minute he stepped out of the rocks right beside me. He was moving so quiet he like to scared me right out of my boots.

"Did you find your friend?"

As soon as I got over my fright enough so I could breathe easy again, I answered him.

"I couldn't see him. But I know he's there. I heard Blake and another man talking about going down to Major Cason's place to collect the ransom money they demanded."

"What about the men in chains?"

"They've got eight men chained up in that big cabin. It's awful, Will. Those men are sleeping on a long platform nailed up to one wall. They're trapped in there with a log chain run through their shackles and hooked up to the walls. Jim could be one of them I reckon. From what I heard, there's a wounded man there somewhere, and I'm assuming that's Jim. They're keeping him in a smaller cabin off to the side."

"Well, that sounds like he's alive at least. That's bound to make you feel a whole lot better."

"You can bet your life it does. I was so relieved when I heard them talking about him I near-about passed out."

"What do we do now?"

"I'll come back up here tomorrow in the daylight. The prisoners will be working the mine then. If Jim is locked in that cabin with the other miners, I wouldn't be able to help him none at night, the way they've got those men chained up. It may be that I'll have to get him out in the daytime.

"Let's get on down to camp and get some sleep, Will. Maybe we can work our way up here tomorrow in a little bit of a roundabout way in the daylight. We could make it look to anybody that sees us like we're trying to shoot us some meat."

Will and me caught the grays and removed their hobbles. As soon as we got mounted Will led the way down the mountain. We moved along as fast as we dared in the dim light.

When we came out of the woods near the lake, I took

the lead and pushed the horses along at a fast walk. I wasn't worried about noise. It seemed to me that most of the men digging for gold during the day oughta be wore out enough to be asleep by now. They shouldn't be too apt to be listening for us.

When we got close to camp I thought I saw a flicker of light over near where I left the buckboard. I pulled my horse to a stop and held my hand out to motion for Will to hold up a minute.

He nodded to indicate that he could see what I was seeing. About that time the light went out. We sat still and watched. A second or two later the light went on again over near the flap of my tent. I was getting just a little bit irritated.

I checked the loads in my handgun and passed it over to Will. I made sure my rifle was ready. Setting the butt of the rifle on my left leg with the barrel straight up in the air, I nodded to Will that I was set. We set our horses to a run and at the same time we commenced to yell like wild Indians, firing the guns in the air.

Roaring into camp with Will right on my heels, I fired at every jump and screamed at the top of my lungs. Will was doing the same thing. It was light enough so I caught a glimpse of two men as they jumped around the tent. They ran like rabbits, ducking out of our sight around behind the wagon.

I jumped down off my horse and fell on my belly behind the tent to yell, "You men drop your guns and come out in the open."

There was no answer. I couldn't see well enough to get a good shot at the men. They musta left their horses tied to the wagon, cause all of a sudden I heard two horses running.

"Well, cuss it all anyway." Will almost spat the words out. He was lying prone, a little off on my left side, holding my pistol in both hands and aiming toward the wagon.

"It's just like the lowdown sneak thieves to run away. I'll bet they were some of the same stinking snakes that killed Pa and took over our claim."

I couldn't help but chuckle at the way the kid was talking. He was sure bloodthirsty. "Just be thankful we got back here when we did. If those varmints were planning on killing us in our sleep they sure came up empty.

"Come on Will, help me check on our supplies before we go to crowing too much about running them varmints away."

I opened the flap to my tent and felt around some. I didn't want to strike a light just yet. I didn't figure I wanted to make myself too good a target in case those men wanted to try again. It looked like we rode in on those two men before they had a chance to bother anything. Everything seemed to be right where I left it.

Will came walking back from behind the wagon.

"How about the wagon, Will? Did they take anything out of there?"

"There wasn't much in there to take, but I checked and I don't think they touched anything."

I figured we were safe enough by then, so I went ahead and struck a match so I could see to really check on the supplies. They were piled up under my cot for safekeeping. Everything looked to be just the way I left it.

"Do you think we should stand guard tonight?" Will asked.

"Yes I do. We should take turns keeping watch for what's left of tonight. Tomorrow morning we'll move most of our supplies and stuff up the hill and hide it in the shaft so it won't be so easy to find if we have visitors again."

"That's a good idea, I think. You want to go back up on the mountain tomorrow, don't you Ken?"

Nodding, I pretended to be busy looking around. I wasn't quite ready yet to tell Will that I wanted him to stay here and act like a miner to give me some cover against whoever was snooping around while I went back up to that mine. When I tell the boy about that notion I might just meet up with some stiff argument. So I hadn't figured out yet just how I wanted to say things.

"I'll take first watch, Will. You go on and get yourself some sleep. I'll give you a shout in a couple of hours."

Will handed me back my pistol without a word and headed for the wagon. From the way he was walking it was easy to tell that the boy was completely wiped out. I figured he'd be asleep the minute his head hit his blanket. Considering what he had been through lately, that was no surprise.

Smoking one cigarette after another, as much to have something to do with my hands as anything, I sat on a blanket in front of my tent and kept watch until dawn. I started out puzzling about what was the best way to help Jim. I ended up dreaming about Meg, remembering the touch of her little hand on my chest. Between my dreaming and planning what to do the time flew. As soon as the sun popped up over the hill I got up and stretched the kinks out.

It came to me that it might be important that I memorize the shape of the footprints left by the men who paid us the midnight visit. I might run across them again someday. After I studied on them for a while I picked up the water bucket and walked down to the lake. I took the time to wash up a little while I was down there, and got a bucket of fresh water for making coffee.

Out in the open like that, it was easy to keep watch down the road and around the lake. Everything looked quiet. When I got back with the fresh water I led the horses down to the lake and let them drink. I led them back to camp and gave them a bait of oats out of the supplies in the buckboard. The sack of oats was looking pretty flat. I knew it was time for me to get moving, for a lot of reasons.

The fire was still smoldering, so I punched it up some and added a little dry wood. It soon got hot enough for me to boil coffee. I could feel the sun on my shoulders when Will finally came out of the wagon. The way he walked made it plain that he was feeling a little bit out of sorts. He held himself stiff like and his face was all drawed up in a scowl.

"Why didn't you call me so I could stand my turn at watch," he said as he came up to the campfire.

He looked and sounded to me like a little kid who didn't get his share of candy. I was really in no mood to argue.

"Get yourself a cup of coffee Will, and forget it." "I couldn't get to sleep so I stayed up. It had nothing to do with you."

The tone of my voice seemed to get the message across. He gave me a hard look, but shut up and poured his coffee. I could tell by his expression that he was pouting because I didn't wake him up so he could do his part. I reckon he thought he had to prove something, but right about then I didn't much care what he thought. I was getting more and more worried about Jim.

We didn't either one of us have anything to say for a while. I fried bacon and mixed up some fry bread to cook in the grease. We ate our breakfast and cleaned up without saying a word.

As soon as we were done with the camp chores I went to move the horses to a spot I had noticed where there was a little more grass for them to eat. The place where I hobbled them was a good distance off to the side of the hill, and not so much out in the open as the last place. The new location would help hide the fact that only one horse was going to be there most of the day.

When I got back over beside the fire I could see that Will had perked himself up a little. I reckon it helped his humor some to get his belly full.

"You know I've got to go back up to that mine and try to get my friend out of there, Will. It would help me if you would stay here on the claim and make noises like you're digging for gold."

"I sort of figured you might say that."

I could tell he wasn't too happy with me by the sound of his voice. He didn't sound like he was mad, just sort of serious and determined.

Will started talking quietly. He sounded almost like he was trying to talk reason to a little kid. "I heard you say something last night about some man with a hurt leg that the woman had been tending. Suppose that man they were talking about turns out to be your friend? Have you thought that if it happens that it is your friend, depending on how bad hurt he is, you're liable to need some help getting him out of there?"

I just sat there and stared at him. I knew I couldn't smack the smart-aleck kid, but I sure wanted to. He was exactly right in what he was saying. I hadn't thought of it at all. If Jim was the wounded man the girl was talking about, I might sure enough need some help getting him out of there.

It was clear to me that I was going to have to re-think what I was fixin' to do. I would have to come up with a whole new plan that would put Will close enough to the mine so he could help me when I needed him, but keep him out of too much danger. It didn't seem possible that two men could sneak in that canyon in the daytime without getting caught, so I abandoned that thought right away. I knew from experience that one of us would have a hard enough time doing it.

"You're right in what you say, Will. I'll have to take you with me. I heard those people saying something about the wounded man's bad leg. If that man is Jim, and by heaven I hope it is, I just don't know what I'll be facing."

Will straightened up and smiled a little then. "I'll go get hackamores on the horses," he said, heading over to the buckboard to get the ropes.

It was a little bit of a relief to see that Will didn't seem to feel too much like crowing. He sure had a right. I guess I was just so excited over thinking Jim was alive after all my worrying that I didn't think things through.

As I kept going over in my head everything I could remember hearing those people say, I had to admit to myself that neither the woman nor the two men had actually said the wounded man was Jim. I just assumed it.

It could be that Jim ain't that man at all, I thought. That thought made me feel so awful I wanted to cry.

We let the grays out some this trip. They were so eager they pulled at the hackamores and when we let them run they moved like they were enjoying themselves. It was almost the middle of the day by the time we finally got out of camp, so I knew people wouldn't think it a bit strange for us to be going up into the woods. If anybody noticed us at all they'd just assume we were going hunting.

Will led the way through the woods again, and I was glad enough to let him do it. I'd have found my way sooner or later, but it woulda taken me a lot longer to follow the tracks we made the night before.

It only took a minute for us to hobble the horses and leave them to graze on the same little patch of grass where we left them last night. I finally talked Will into staying with the horses again, so he could go for help if he heard a ruckus or I didn't make it back by the time we agreed.

We made a deal that he would come up to the rocks and look in the canyon if I was up there for more than four hours. We had messed around camp so long before we started out that it would be near-about dark by that time. If he looked in there and couldn't see me nowhere, he was to go down to Belden and get Miss Hetty fired up to come rescue me.

Chapter Six

After all my thinking and puzzling, I came to the conclusion that if I couldn't find a way to get Jim out of there in four hours I probably ought to just get myself out of the place anyway. If it come to that, Will and me would both ride down to Belden and get us some help. That was a scary thing to even think about though.

I was pretty certain that if anybody started to raid that camp the first thing that would happen is those crooks would kill Jim and hide his body. They would almost be forced to do that to cover their tracks. If those other prisoners Blake had chained in that cabin were the disappearing miners, and I truly believed they were, the crooks would surely kill them too.

It would be awkward, but I decided to take my rifle with me this trip. I thought I might get in a fix where I would need all the firepower I could get. When I got to the top of the rocks, I noticed that the door of the big cabin where they chained the prisoners up at night was standing wide open. I couldn't see a guard standing anywhere near the buildings.

I caught sight of several men working in some rocks across the canyon, right up near the opening to the mine,

but they were much too far away for me to tell if Jim was
in the group.

After watching the camp a minute or two, I decided
everything was as clear as it ever would be. I turned and
waved my hand to let Will know I was going. Then I
scrambled over the crest of the hill and down the slope.
Moving as quietly as I could, I nudged and scooted myself
in behind the rocks at the bottom. I lay still a few minutes
to make sure no one had spotted me.

After a bit I got up and hunched down low to run toward
the little patch of aspens. All I could do was hope that
nobody from the camp would happen to look my way before I was under cover.

I made it into the patch of trees without anybody throwing lead at me, so I assumed nobody knew I was in the
canyon. I crouched down and waited a minute or two to
see if I could hear somebody giving an alarm. All I could
hear was the irregular clanging of steel sledgehammers hitting against rock and a deep rumbling-grinding sound I
couldn't identify.

When I decided it was safe to move, I set out to find the
other end of the little grove of aspens. I knew there was
bound to be a regular entrance to this box canyon, one that
would accommodate horses at least, if not a wagon. I
wanted to find it. That would surely be the way Blake and
his men used to go in and out of the place. I wanted to
know more about the layout of the whole canyon before I
started nosing around up close to the cabins in the daylight.

Stopping and waiting a second or two after each step, I
kept listening for any change in the sounds that were coming from the mine. The aspens were bare, and their trunks
were much too small for me to really hide behind, but there
were a few clumps of serviceberry bushes that would help
to confuse the eye of anybody that happened to be looking
my way.

I didn't have to go far before I could see the edge of a rough track running along past the edge of the aspens. Beyond the road was a sheer rock wall that looked to be sixty or seventy feet high. I craned my neck back and looked almost straight up to see the top. I couldn't help but wonder how anybody ever found this place. It was a perfect hideout. Blake probably found it by accident, the same way Will did.

Staying well back in the trees to get as much cover as possible, I slowly worked my way around toward the sound of the sledgehammers. The little patch of trees wasn't more than a couple of hundred yards long. When I came near the upper end of the aspens, I stretched out on the ground and pushed up close against a thick clump of those serviceberry bushes for cover. I could see the men working up in the rocks fairly well from where I was. If Jim was one of them it would be easy to spot him.

Two men stood guard over the miners. One carried a Greener hanging across his left arm. I assumed he was the same man I saw guarding the prisoners' cabin last night. He appeared to be about the same height and shape. I wondered if that meant he only guarded the prisoners for a few hours each night. He would surely need to sleep sometime.

The big man beside him was carrying a wide leather strap attached to a wooden handle. It hung down from his right hand so far it skimmed the ground when he walked.

I took him to be the man called Don that was with Blake in the cabin last night. He kept swinging the whip-thing around. About every other swing he would whack it up against a rock. It made an awful sound. I almost felt like cringing every time I heard it. I had read about whipping bosses on plantations back in slavery days, but I never expected to actually see one.

Taking my time so I could be as thorough as possible, I examined each of the prisoners carefully, trying to spot Jim.

It was hard to get a good look at the faces of the men when they were busy swinging the big hammers, but I could easily eliminate most of them by their shape.

I finally noticed a man riding a mule around in circles over near the entrance to the opening of a new-looking mine shaft. The mule was pulling the guide log on a small crusher mill. The mill looked like it worked the same way as one the Mexicans used to use. That was the way they crushed silver ore. It's kind of a mill that pulverizes the small pieces of ore like the ones the prisoners were smashing up. That's how they got the mineral out. I think the name of the thing is an arrastrae.

The first thing I noticed about the man sitting up on the mule was his right leg had been tied up in splints. The bandages went all the way up to his knee. Then I realized he had red hair hanging down in his collar.

The sight of that red hair made me want to yell out loud. *It was Jim Cason up on that mule, sure as death.* I was so glad to see him I felt a sob push up in my throat. I had to wipe my eyes before I could look again.

When the mule came around so faced toward me, I could see that Jim was sort of slumped over, like he was tired or in pain or something. I felt my face flush and went to thinking about how much I really wanted to hurt somebody over this mess.

While I was studying on what to do next, I kept thinking *I was hearing some sort of sound behind me that didn't belong.* I looked over my shoulder a couple of times, but I never could see anything. Then I realized that at least part of what I was hearing was the sound of two horses coming up the road beside the aspens.

I lay stretched flat out on the ground, hoping nobody would see me. Ideas were bouncing around in my head. I knew I had to find a way to get Jim out of here and up on one of those gray horses.

When the two men on the horses came into sight they

rode right on through the camp and around behind the big cabin. Evidently there was a corral back there somewhere, because presently the same two men walked back to where I could see them. They kept on down toward the cabin where I watched the woman and the two men the night before.

I raised myself up on my knees so I could see the men better. I was wondering if there was any way I could get close enough to hear what they had to say when all of a sudden my head felt like it was split in two pieces. The next second everything went black.

When I came to myself again, I wasn't sure where I was. Nothing I could see looked the least bit familiar. Finally, it must have been about the third time I opened my eyes, I figured out that I was lying on a bunk inside a small cabin.

I could hear voices, somebody talking real soft. It sounded like they were somewhere real close to me. My head was hurting so much I couldn't concentrate enough to make out anything they were saying. I closed my eyes against the pain and I guess I passed out again.

After a while I began to wake up and notice things. The cabin was quiet. Whoever it was that was talking earlier was evidently gone. I couldn't hear anything. The pain in my head finally settled down enough for me to risk opening my eyes. My vision was blurred, and I had to strain, but I could see there was somebody lying on a pallet across the room from me.

I think whoever hit me must have busted my head a little, because it took me forever to realize I was looking right at Jim Cason. I tried to raise myself up, but when I did, I found out I was tied down tight against the bunk. There were ropes across my whole body and all the way down my legs.

Looking around as much as I could, I couldn't see anybody else in the room so I called out, "Jim—Jim Cason."

Jim sat straight up real quick and shook his head at me.

Barely whispering, he said, "Keep your voice down, old man. We don't want Blake to find out you're awake just yet."

I nodded, then wished I hadn't. The movement made pains shoot down my neck and up the back of my head.

"Talk low, Ken. But tell me how in blue blazes you got yourself caught by these crooks." Jim whispered.

"That was easy," I said, resting my aching head back against the mattress. "I was looking for my pard so hard I set myself out there for the pickin' and one of them took me up on it."

"How did you ever find this place?"

"You ain't the only friend I've got, you know."

"Be serious, you idiot."

"Another friend of mine told me about it. He found it when he was hunting. He heard those prisoners knocking around on rocks with their sledgehammers and climbed up on the top of those rocks to take a look. He didn't have no way of knowing Blake was holding anybody like you a prisoner here. He didn't tell anybody what he saw because his Pa told him the men held up here in chains were probably a county convict crew Blake had hired."

I looked out of the corner of my eye to keep from jarring my head again and I could see Jim shaking his head.

"Get serious, Ken. These people are as vicious as wolverines. Every single one of the men they've got chained up out yonder came from that mining operation they're working down on my place."

"That ape Blake refers to as Don used to be a whipping-boss in a chain gang camp over at the territorial prison. I know you remember hearing that some of the roads going out of Denver were built by crews made up of prisoners. Well, that Don fella's running himself a regular convict camp up here, only these prisoners aren't criminals at all, they're just regular miners that he and Blake's other men kidnapped right off the road to Belden."

"How in the world do they capture the men?"

"The one named Don and two of the other guards waylay them and hold them up when they're leaving the diggings. Some of the miners are just going down to town to send money home or go to the saloon or something. They steal their gold, their outfits, and their stock. They bring the men they don't kill up here to this place. They lock those chains on 'em and put 'em to work in the mine."

"How did they get you, Jim? What happened to your leg?"

I was feeling more than anxious. My head was hurting bad enough to make me want to cry. I wasn't sure I could even think straight, but I was certainly thinking clear enough to know we had to figure out a way to get out of there fast.

I must have sounded funny when I talked, because Jim sounded real concerned about me.

"You take it slow now Ken, you had a nasty knock on your head. It's a good thing it's so thick, I reckon. We're not going anywhere for a while yet. I'm working on something, but it all depends on Blake's girl helping me. She wants to get away from here herself."

"You mean that young woman that works in the mine office?"

"Her name is Jenny Drumheller. She'll be up here with our supper in a little while and I'll introduce her to you. Jenny's a good girl, but she hasn't had it easy what with her getting left to live with Blake. She's Blake's stepdaughter. Her mother died over in Colorado Springs last year, and she's been stuck with Blake ever since. I promised to take her out of here with me and pay her train fare to Chicago. She wants to go there to live with her mother's sister."

"Are you sure you can trust her to help us?"

"As sure as I can be of another person. She'll help us

any way she can, Ken. She wants out of here too. You'll see. You wait 'til you meet her."

"Tell me what happened to you."

"You know how I enjoy fishing. Well, it sort of got to be a habit with me to go fishing down by the lake early mornings. I'd been down there for about an hour one morning when I looked up to see five riders coming down the hill toward me. It so happened that right at that minute my rifle was leaning against a rock about twenty feet away from me.

"You can bet I cussed myself some for being a fool. I hadn't even thought to put a handgun on. It had been so peaceful up here ever since you left that I never even thought of needing to have a handgun on when I was just going to sit out by the lake and fish. At least not right at the crack of dawn.

"I didn't like the looks of the riders off for some reason. I stood up and started moving real easy to get myself over closer to my rifle. Before I got to standing up good that Blake pulled out his pistol and shot me in the leg.

"He never even said a word, Ken. He just drew his pistol and shot me."

"That's the awfulest thing I've ever heard of."

"Yeah, well, it was awful all right."

"What happened then?"

"Right at first, it felt like the bullet took my whole leg right off. Blood started pouring down. The bullet made a hole in my leg about six inches below my knee and it knocked me down flat."

"When I got over the shock a little, I sat there on the ground and took my belt off to make me a tourniquet. I knew that bleeding needed to be stopped as quick as possible. It was pouring down my leg."

"About that time the woman, Jenny that is, jumped off her horse and ran over to help me. I didn't know her name then, of course. She pushed my hand out of the way and pulled a scarf from around her neck. She got that tied around my leg and found a stick to twist it tight. I was almost passing out from the pain by that time. My leg was a real mess.

"As soon as she stopped my leg from bleeding so much, Jenny turned around to look up at Blake and said, 'You've done it now. The bone in his leg is broken. It's going to take a time for it to heal.'

"I was awake enough to understand what she said and it some kind of upset me, you can bet on that. My leg was hurting me so much by that time I was almost out of it. I can't remember everything that happened there for a while, but I do remember thinking that if my leg was permanently crippled I might as well be dead.

"Blake pushed his horse over close beside me. He didn't say anything at first. His eyes looked so cold that for a minute or two there I thought he was going to shoot me— just go ahead and put me out of my misery like you would a horse with a broken leg. But he just stared down at me for a minute or two then he turned his head and spoke to the woman.

"'Tie his leg up tight Jenny, and help him on your horse so we can get him up to that cabin. He's going to tell us where he got that top-grade gold ore he brought over to the assay office in Colorado Springs.' "

I interrupted, "Gold, what gold? I didn't know you had found gold up here," wondering how many other secrets Jim was keeping.

"Yeah, I found me an old abandoned mine. It was one day when I was out hunting. It must have been a couple of weeks after you left out of here. I came back down to the cabin and got me a pick and a good lantern and came back up here to nose around."

"First I checked a shaft that was partly blocked with boulders. I threw a couple of rocks as far back in it as I could, but it must be really deep. I could just barely hear a sound when the rocks hit bottom. I gave up on that one right away. It sounded like a death trap to me."

"What did you do then?"

"I nosed around and found another shaft over to the west of the first one. Its opening was covered over by heavy growth, but when I cleared that away the shaft was still clear. It went straight back on a level. The ceiling looked to be solid rock, so I decided to explore some.

"When I got to the end of the shaft there were some old tools lying around. They were all corroded and rusty and the handles were rotting away. It was easy to see that they had been there for a long, long time. There was a wide streak of rose quartz right across the end of the workings. I held up my light to study it and doggoned if I couldn't see some traces of color."

"Do you think somebody just abandoned it?"

"It looked to me like somebody simply dropped their tools and walked away and never came back. It's hard to imagine what happened to cause them to do such a thing. I figure whoever it was must have abandoned it many years ago, from the shape the tools were in."

"Had you ever heard anybody say there was gold up here?" I asked.

"I've never heard it, have you?"

"It's news to me. Tell me what you did after you found the mine."

"From the looks of the quartz at the end of the tunnel I thought it might be worth working that shaft some. I had me a good feeling about it. I kept going to the mine and digging around for a few hours as often as I could spare the time over the next few weeks."

"I found me some promising-looking pieces of quartz, so I gathered up the best looking ones in a flour sack and rode over to Colorado Springs to have them assayed. I didn't want to bring them down to Belden. I was afraid I'd start a gold rush if the ore panned out to be high grade."

"That's sure enough what happened when that Blake took over your place." I said. "You ought to see the crowd of would-be miners piled up in that town. I couldn't hardly ride or walk through the street the other day."

"I was going to tell you about the mine when I came down to town to get me some more supplies, Ken. I got a few of the supplies I needed when I was over to Colorado Springs to see the assayer, but I was beginning to run low on just about everything again when this thing happened.

"Well, let me get back to the story of how I ended up lying here in this cabin. I must have passed out completely about the time Blake was standing over me down there by the lake. When I came to myself again I was sitting astride Jenny's horse and my leg was hurting like the devil. I clearly remember looking down at the blood still pouring out through my pants leg and running into my boot, and everything went black again. I guess I really fainted then."

"It was pitch dark when I woke up. These same handcuffs right here were on my wrists. I was completely confused at first, but I kept looking and thinking until I eventually figured out that I was lying in my cabin on my own bunk. The handcuffs were a mystery. I lay there and sort of went in and out of consciousness for a while.

"The next morning I came awake enough to understand that the three men and Jenny had obviously spent the night in the cabin. The woman was stirring the fire and making coffee. She finally brought a cup over to me.

"She told me her name then, and explained that the bullet had broken a small bone in my leg. She'd stopped the bleeding and bound my leg up with some splints to hold it steady. The hurting had settled down to a dull ache by that time.

"I asked her what was going on, but before she could answer me Blake and the two other men came in the cabin. The two men went on to the table to eat their breakfast, but Blake came over to stand by the bunk and stare down at me with those cold-fish eyes again.

"He didn't say hello, go to the devil, or anything. He just said I was going to tell him where my gold mine was or he was going to let one of his friends cut my hurt leg off at the knee."

"My Lord. What did you say to him?"

"I told him where he could go, of course. I thought he was just bullying me. It never occurred to me to believe he really would do such a thing. He looked down at me and laughed out loud, then walked over to the table to get his own breakfast.

"Later on, when the men left the cabin, Jenny told me that Blake was her stepfather and she wanted to get away from him and go live with some of her mother's people. She promised that if I cooperated with the men about the gold she would help me get away from them as soon as I was able to travel.

"She asked me to promise her that if she helped me I would help her get away from Blake. It seems her mother was married to Blake, but she died of consumption a few months back. Jenny said she knew she wasn't safe with Blake and his men. She wanted to go to live with her mother's sister in Chicago.

"Jenny also explained that Blake meant every word he said about cutting my leg off. She claimed he would order that Don fella to take a saw or maybe an axe and cut my leg right off, for a fact."

"You don't mean she really believed he would do such a thing?"

"According to her Blake and the men with him were so vicious and mean that if they didn't get their way they would do anything. They didn't care about nothing or no-body. She swore she had once seen her stepfather, that Blake, cut a man's hand off with an axe in a fight over a card game.

"Then Jenny explained that she had told them that my leg would get better in a few weeks so I would be able to work. She knew that if they thought they could get some work out of me they would keep me alive. They were gonna need men to work in my mine. She had heard them planning on how they would get at the gold once they forced me to tell them how to find it."

"That Don came back in the cabin later on that same night carrying my axe in one hand. He came over to stand by the bunk and grin down at me. He looked about as scary as one of those evil Kachina dolls the Indians sometimes make.

"He held the axe up on his shoulder and stared at me for a minute or two. I thought he was going to chop my leg off right that minute. He finally walked over to prop the axe up in the corner across the room from me.

"I told Blake I'd show them where my mine was. I didn't want them to even begin to get the idea that I was hard to get along with. Not while I was lying there helpless.

"They waited around at the cabin one more day, then dragged me out and put me on a horse. I led them up here and showed them how to find my gold, and I'm doggoned glad I did it. What I've seen them do and heard them order done to men since I've been up here has made it plain what they would do to get what they want."

"What do you mean by that?"

"There was one big guy they brought in here tied across the back of a mule. I didn't see it, of course, cause I was shut up in here, but Jenny told me what happened. When they threw the man off the mule down to the ground he jumped up and started to run down the road. They had already put shackles on his legs and arms, but he ran the best he could anyway.

"Blake stood there and watched the man struggle along for a minute or two, then he motioned to that henchman of his that carries the Greener around all the time. That sorry excuse for a human being walked out in the middle of the road and shot the poor man in both legs with that shotgun.

"The other two guards walked over to pick him up by his arms and dragged him back along the road past the aspens. I didn't know what was going on until later, but I could hear the poor man screaming. Jenny said the two guards dropped him over into a deep ravine. It's over on the far side of that road that runs around the rock wall across from the aspens."

"I can't hardly believe it."

"That ain't the worst of it yet, Ken. The sounds was faint, but I swear I could hear that poor man screaming off and on for two days after that."

"For God's sake, Jim. What kind of people are they?"

"They're not much better than rabid dogs, in my way of thinking, Ken. Make no mistake about it. Those men could take a notion to walk in here and kill us both at any time. They don't need a reason, either."

We both got quiet then. It was almost too much for a normal person to get his head around. How could human men do such things to other men? It was beyond hard for me to understand. Somehow, it made it worse for me to know they were doing it all for gold.

A dozen questions I needed to ask Jim kept buzzing around in my mind, but my head was hurting me so much it was just too painful for me to keep on talking. Every time I figured out the words to use to say something, I would feel the pain and lose them again.

I guess I fell asleep after that, because some small sound woke me. I looked around to see the young woman I talked to in the mine office coming through the cabin door. She was carrying a tray with some bowls and cups on it in one hand. A little basket was hanging from the same arm. She stopped in the doorway and looked over at me for a minute.

I thought I saw recognition in her eyes and something else I couldn't figure out. I don't know why, but I had the crazy thought that she looked glad to see me.

The woman walked over and put the tray down on a packing box sitting next to Jim's pallet then she bent over to help him sit up. Handing him one of the bowls and a cup, she took a loaf of bread out of the basket and broke it in half, giving Jim one piece and putting the other piece down on the tray.

I strained to hear what she was saying to Jim. She was speaking almost too softly for me to make out the words.

"Have you been able to talk to your friend yet? Is he going to be all right?"

"I think he's going to be all right, Jenny. He's an old iron head anyway. I've been telling him that ever since we were boys. Don't you worry none about him."

"Blake said he was going to come up here in a little while and hold a gun on him while he eats his supper, then he's going to chain him so he can put him to work in the mine tomorrow."

"We need to delay that some if we possibly can."

"I'll run back down yonder to the other cabin and tell Blake that the new prisoner hasn't come back to his senses yet."

"That's a good idea. You go ahead and do that, Jenny. It should work. I expect Ken's hungry, but I know he's not near hungry enough to trade food for having chains locked around his arms and legs."

"Well, they won't really be doing that anyway. Not until they get some more chains or another one of the miners dies. They used up all of the shackles they brought with them. They had to use ropes on the last two men they brought in instead of those iron things."

"Good, that means that even if he does come up here and take Ken over to the other cabin he'll still have some chance of working himself loose of the ropes and getting away."

The woman didn't say any more after that. She picked up the tray with the food that was intended for me and went out the door. I figured it was just as well. I probably couldn't eat anything anyway, the way I was feeling.

I watched the expression on Jim's face as the woman left the cabin. It seemed like he was looking at her kinda like I had seen him looking at Millie. That made me wonder if he was maybe falling in love with Jenny or something like. If I would've been feeling a mite better I mighta gotten mad.

"Ken?" I heard Jim calling me as if from a distance.

"Hey, Ken?" He called again.

I finally roused myself up enough to answer him. I couldn't get out a word. My answer came out as sort of a grunt.

He wasn't much more than whispering, "Act like you're still knocked out, Ken. I think I hear Blake and another man coming up this way. They're likely coming to check up on you."

Sure enough, it wasn't even a minute later until I heard the padlock sort of clank against the hasp on the door. The hinges creaked as the door was pushed open. I closed my eyes and tried to completely relax my whole body. I could feel the cot vibrate as their heavy steps crossed the floor. A hand caught me by my leg and shook me, hard. I wanted to groan out loud, the shaking made my poor head hurt me so bad, but I managed not to react.

I figured it was Blake who spoke. His voice sounded different, because he was so close to me, but I thought I recognized it from the other night.

"I guess Jenny knew what she was talking about. This man's out like a candle in a norther.

"You must have hit him one heck of a blow with that pistol of yours, Oscar. I've told you before to ease up on these men a little bit. You don't need to be so blasted hard on them. We really do need some more workers in the mine. If you've broken this one's head by hitting him too hard, we'll be running a dratted hospital for him too, just like for this Cason fella here. That is, if we ever expect him to be able to do any work for us."

I lay there pretending to be completely out of it, but I was wishing as hard as I ever wished for anything in my life that I had me a gun, a knife, or maybe even a dirty, rusty pitchfork. Lord a mercy, how I itched to see those lowdown, filthy, sidewinders bleed.

I was thinking straight enough by then to know it was my imagination, but it seemed like I could smell the evil coming off those two men. The man I assumed was Blake spoke to the other man, who sort of grunted in response. I heard Blake walk across the room toward Jim before he started talking again.

"How about you, Cason? Are you ready to work hard and pay me back for keeping you alive all these weeks?"

"Oh, I'm getting better fast now, Captain Blake," Jim said.

I don't know how he did it, but Jim was speaking to that man in a nice, friendly-sounding voice.

"My leg still hurts me something fierce when I try to rest my full weight on it, but Jenny says she can probably take these infernal splints off me by the end of the week."

"Well, I'll go by what Jenny says about that. I need that ore broken up so it can be crushed. So I need both of you men to be able to work. When I leave Shell Mountain I plan to take enough gold with me so I'll never have to worry about money again for the rest of my life."

Blake just kept on talking as if he thought we would be interested.

"The whole idea of living high in Paris or London is giving me a really good feeling toward just about everybody. Why, I might even decide to leave the whole bunch

of you men alive when I ride out of here. That is, if you
work hard enough at getting the gold out for me until that
day comes. Of course, I'm not at all sure leaving you alive
is exactly what the rest of my men hold in mind for you
fellas." Blake sort of chuckled when he said that.

"I guess I'll have to leave that up to the men. They might
not be planning on leaving the country like I am. I don't
expect any of those men would be comfortable living in
Paris or London, not even if you include old Oscar here.

"They might be planning on crossing the border into
Mexico, but if they aren't leaving the country, it could be
that they might be worried that if they leave you two cow-
pokes alive one of you might remember their faces someday.

"When I think of that I'm obliged to admit, I don't know
what they'll want to do with you. Oscar here and old Don
can both be downright vindictive at times. In fact, I sometimes think they rather enjoy hurting people.

"I've even been having a hard time convincing Don that
your Pa would really pay out good money to save your
sorry hide, Cason. There's been a couple of times he argued
with me that taking care of you was just too much trouble.
I think he really wanted to drop you in the arroyo like they
did a couple of other miners that were a little unfortunate."

I was lying there betting to myself that Jim was smoldering. He was bound to be mad as fire. That was about
the most lowering thing I ever experienced in my life—to
have to hear Blake taunting Jim like that and me lying here
as helpless as a day-old kitten.

"I'm sure the Major will have the money ready that you
asked for, Captain Blake. I know he's good for it." Jim
said. "Didn't you tell him in the note you left that you were
going to trade me for the cash?"

Blake and the other man both started laughing out loud.

Blake didn't even bother to answer Jim. I heard the their heavy footsteps cross the floor and go out the door. The skunks were still laughing as they locked the door and walked away.

Chapter Seven

I raised my head a little and looked over at Jim. His face was chalky white. That was a sure sign he was madder than a stepped-on rattler. Jim always did that. When we were boys, whenever Jim went white and got really quiet he was getting ready to break out in a blind fury.

"Easy Jim," I whispered.

"I'm going to get my chance at those low-down pieces of no-good, filthy, stable-scrapings." Jim said softly.

"We'll both get a chance at 'em, boy." I whispered.

"I hope you're right."

"When is this woman going to help us get out of here?"

"Jenny told me earlier today that Blake and that Don are riding down to Pa's place about dark tonight to collect the ransom money. She said Blake sent somebody down to the ranch sometime last night or early this morning with a note telling Pa where he should leave it."

My head was hurting something fierce from so much talking and listening and thinking. I closed my eyes to keep out the light. That seemed to make the pain ease up a little bit.

I guess I went to off to sleep again. I dreamt that Will

Davis rode down to Belden and found Meg and led her up here to get Jim and me out of this mess. It seemed to me like I could see Meg riding a big black horse and wearing Tom Dillard's star.

A loud banging woke me up. It about scared me half to death. It felt like something really big hit the side of the cabin. The dim light coming in through the little window was throwing long shadows across the room. It was so dark I knew it had to be night outside.

When the door opened two men sort of shoved or maybe they threw another person into the cabin. I could see well enough to tell that whoever it was had his arms pulled around behind him and tied. His legs were tied together too. He landed with a thump on the floor over close to Jim's pallet.

Neither one of the men who threw him in the room said a word. They turned around as soon as they dropped the tied-up fella, walked out of the cabin and slammed the door. I heard them put the lock back on the door before they left.

The man on the floor struggled until he could sit up. He shook his head a couple of times as he looked around. He sort of cleared his throat some and asked, "Is that you up on that bunk Ken?"

I thought my heart would surely stop beating when I heard that voice. I was really feeling down all of a sudden. My ace-in-the-hole had turned out to be worth nothing at all. The man those crooks had thrown on the floor was a boy named William Tell Davis. Somehow those filthy, sneaking weasels had managed to capture him. My dream about Meg rescuing us was exactly that. A wild dream.

"What the Sam Hill happened to you, Will?"

I tried hard, but I couldn't keep the disappointment from coming through in my voice.

Will's voice sounded kind of shaky when he answered.

"I was sitting there giving you just a little bit more time to get yourself out of here, Ken, when all of a sudden somebody grabbed me from behind."

"Doggone it all anyway," I said.

I hoped Will wasn't crying. *I* sure didn't have the patience for that.

"What about the horses, Will, what happened to the horses?"

"They got one of them. But the geldings didn't like those two men one little bit, Ken. They got hold of both of the horses at first. Then they decided they were going to ride them. They tied me up and threw me over the back of one of their mounts.

"Then one of the men tried to put his saddle up on the gelding's back but the horse fought him so hard he knocked the man and his saddle down on the ground. Before either of the men could get their hands on him again that horse ran down the mountain. I saw him go in the woods."

It was easy for me to commence to worrying hard about our situation at that point. With Will captured we were left dependent on that Jenny woman to give us even the smallest chance of getting out of there. I couldn't stop a little thought from sneaking in my head that I should be saying *getting out of there alive*.

If the gelding ran all the way to Aunt Hetty's she would get help and come looking for me, but she wouldn't know where to go or what to do. These people would kill us for sure if anybody from outside came charging up here. Anybody that knew what was really going on would sneak in and catch them unawares. Then they wouldn't have time to get rid of the evidence—us that is.

Jim hadn't said a word since Will was thrown in the cabin, but I knew he was awake. I kept my voice low and called to him, "Do you think it's possible that woman can help three of us get out of this place Jim?"

I heard Jim sort of choke back a chuckle as he answered. "We'll just have to make a try at it, won't we?"

"What the heck are you laughing about?" I demanded. I was feeling sort of aggravated. Be blest if I could see any reason for merriment.

"I want to know how anybody ever saw this kid in the dark. *He's as black as my* favorite Morgan horse."

"Now Jim, you behave yourself."

I didn't know if Will might get his feelings hurt at Jim's teasing. As it turned out, I needn't have worried.

Jim's humor didn't faze Will. He came right back at him, real sharp.

"It was those infernal almost white horses they spotted, or I'd a been perfectly safe. They were kind of gleaming in the bright moonlight. When they crept up close enough to grab hold of them is when they got close enough to see me."

Jim chuckled again. "Howdy there Will, I'm Jim Cason. I reckon this broken down old cowpoke has told you about me?"

"You're why we're both here," Will answered. He still sounded kind of smart-alecky, I thought.

"When I met Ken he was sitting beside his campfire moping and worrying about you for some crazy reason."

"Hey, hold it there. You two can throw insults around another day. That is, if we ever get out of the fix we're in." I couldn't help but speak kind of sharp like. I was beginning to feel a little bit impatient with both of the silly jokers.

"Jim, when is that woman going to help us?"

"You get ahold to your patience, Ken." Jim said, sounding kind of short-tempered his own self.

"Jenny will come through. She'll be up here sometime later tonight. She had to wait until she knew Blake would be away from here for a few hours."

Jim's voice got sort of hard then. "I think you better stop and thank your lucky stars we have a friend like her instead of questioning her."

"You're right, Jim. I'm sorry to be so cranky. My head feels like it's about broke in two, and drat it all, I need the backhouse.

"Don't you two clowns dare laugh at me, either."

I think it was Will I heard snickering then. I just turned my head to the wall and tried to ignore the both of them.

I may have dozed some more after that, but I know I didn't go sound asleep again because I heard light footsteps outside just before the door opened. Jenny stepped in, toting a small bundle wrapped in what looked like a blanket. She put the bundle down beside the door and ran over to Jim.

"Here's a bowie knife, Jim, it's the only weapon I could get. Hurry up and cut your friend loose and let's get the heck out of here. We don't dare try to get horses. Oscar and the other guards are up in their shack playing cards. They'll hear us for sure if we try to get to the corral. We'll have plenty of time, and it's beginning to rain again now. Blake won't be able to track us."

The first thing I heard was the sound of the stick that was sitting beside Jim's bed as it clunked against the floor. He was upright and moving on his own, but he had to lean on the stick to walk. I got a sort of sinking feeling as I thought of him trying to make it through the woods all the way down to my camp leaning on that thing and having his hands chained together.

Jim came across the room to stand beside me. He made short work of the ropes that were holding me down with that bowie knife. Balancing himself against the stick, he took hold of my arm and pulled me up so I could sit on the side of the bunk. My head went to spinning again as soon as I got straightened up.

He left me sitting there trying to get my bearings and stumped over to cut the ropes off Will's wrists and ankles. Will rubbed his wrists as he came over to help get me up on my feet.

Jenny was peeping through a crack in the door.

"I think it's all clear out there, I can't see anybody. I heard Blake and Don riding down the road past the aspens a few minutes before I started out."

Now Jim Cason has a way of taking over anything he gets involved in if you let him. I reckon he took that after his Pa. I was feeling so everlasting poorly that this was one time I was happy to let him do it. He nodded in approval when he saw that Will was sort of propping me up.

Jim swung his crude crutch around and led the way out of the cabin door. He moved surprisingly fast on cleared ground and was halfway to the trees when Jenny closed the cabin door behind us and put the padlock back in place.

Will and me headed for the woods as fast as I could move. When we got well back into the aspens the girl motioned for us all to sit down on the ground. Jenny left us there and crept across to the edge of the road to watch down the hill. After two or three minutes she turned and came back to where we were waiting.

"It's quiet, and I can't see anybody coming up the road. Blake shouldn't be back for two or three hours at least, and I've never known anyone else to ride up here. I think we should try for the pines outside the canyon, if you're feeling up to it, Jim."

"You bet your life I feel up to it." Jim said.

"Don't feel like you have stand around and wait for me, Ken. I'll make it. You take Jenny and run."

"I'm not going to leave you, old son." I said.

Latching onto Will, I used him as a crutch. He pulled on my arm and helped me up to my feet again. As soon as I was standing up, Will nodded to Jenny and we started walking toward the road. We were sure a sorry sight—me hanging on to Will and Jim hanging on to Jenny to keep from falling down.

It must have been the cold air I was breathing in, but I got to feeling almost human again right quick like. There was a fresh breeze blowing up that smelled like rain. We hadn't gone but a few steps when the buzzing was gone out of my head and I was getting to feel steady again.

As soon as my head cleared some I started to think about those men sleeping in that cabin back there with that log chain holding them down. It was looking like we'd probably all be able to get away from here clean. Even with Jim's leg slowing us down I was sure we'd get far enough down the mountain before Blake came back and found us gone so he couldn't catch us.

The rub was I was almost sure that when Blake found out we had escaped he would kill those miners. He would have to do something to keep them from talking about what had been done to them. The way I was seeing it, our escaping would be good for us, no question, but it would be the same as signing a death warrant for those men locked up in that cabin.

"Hold on here a minute folks," I said as I yanked my arm out of Will's hands. I stopped walking.

"What is it?" Will asked.

"I'm feeling okay now. You three go on ahead. I've got to go back and see if I can free those men that are chained down in that big cabin. If we just leave here now Blake and his men are gonna kill them for sure as soon as he comes back and finds us gone."

"Ken, don't be a fool. You're still reeling from that blow on your head." Jim whispered, sounding impatient.

"You can't do anything to help those men. You're not even armed."

"You and Will get Jenny out of here, Jim. You promised her you would, and I want Will someplace where he'll be safe too. He's too young to be taking chances on getting caught by men like these."

"I am not too young."

Will was sounding like a little kid again.

"Look, I'm going back, and I'm going alone, so you can both forget it." I whispered. "Maybe I can find some sort of a weapon. I'm planning on trying to slip up on those guards and put them out of commission one by one."

Jenny pushed in between Will and Jim to look up at me. "I've got the bowie. You go ahead and take it."

"It's a darn shame you couldn't have gotten us a pistol at least." Jim said, unnecessarily.

"I wanted to, Jim, but Blake has all the guns they took from the prisoners in a big trunk in the cabin. The only reason I was able to get the Bowie knife is I was using it to cut bacon. It must have belonged to one of those men they took prisoner down at the diggings, but Blake gave it to me to use because it was sharp and cut better than my old one did. I reckon he forgot I had it.

"The trunk Blake keeps all of those extra weapons in is always kept locked up tight. Blake won't let anyone but himself get near it. I don't know if he suspected I might help one of you escape if I could get my hands on a gun or if he was just naturally extra careful."

Jenny knelt down to untie the old blanket that held her belongings and rummaged around for the bowie knife. It was old and the sheath looked about to fall to pieces, but when she took it out it looked well cared for, and a touch proved that the blade was sharp.

I reached out and took the knife out of her hand. "I thank you, ma'am. I'll take it. It looks fine to me."

"Ken, you've got to use some sense." Jim's tone sounded serious. "If you're going back in there, somebody's got to go with you."

"No Jim. You're not up to it and Will's not going with me. I won't have it," I said, shaking my head.

"Get yourselves out of here like I tell you. There has to be somebody outside of this place that knows what's going on. Will was supposed to be doing that for me when Blake's men slipped up on him. The only real help either one of you can be right now is to stay outside where you can get ahold of somebody with enough firepower to come in here and finally break up this nest of crooks."

"Suppose one of the men Blake left here to guard the place catches you sneaking around? What would you do then?" Will asked, still whispering.

Jim chimed in, "Blake and his sidekick will surely get back here before we can get to Belden and round up a posse. I'm so slow pulling myself along on this stick it could take us hours."

"Stop worrying about me and just go, you two. Time's–a–wasting."

Will touched my arm and said, "You go ahead and let me stay and help you, Ken. Jim and Miss Jenny can get out of here and bring the law back."

"Thank you, Will, I know you want to help. But the best way you can help me is to get Jim out of here. He'll never make it on his own and Jenny's not strong enough to support him for that distance. Jim needs to be there when you or Jenny get to Belden so he can convince the sheriff and other folks to hurry."

Will looked a little mulish, but he could see the logic of what I was saying to him. He finally nodded his head.

Jim didn't say anymore either. He gave me a hard look and reached out to land a slap on my shoulder. Then he motioned for Will to pick up Jenny's bundle and turned to start hobbling downhill.

I stood there for a minute or two until they were far enough away to be lost in the gloom. I knew Jim would act smart and keep them far enough back in the woods where they could hide if they heard somebody coming along the track. He would take a path parallel to the road, and use it as a guide.

Will and Jenny were walking on either side of Jim when they went out of sight. It felt good knowing that Will was with them. He's young I know, but he's big and strong. Jim was going to need a lot of help before he got himself down to town with that cast on his leg. The boy and Jenny would help him along when he got worn out from swinging that infernal stick.

Chapter Eight

The edge on the bowie was razor sharp. When I thought about it a little, I had a sort of sinking feeling that I might not be able to put it to its best use. There was no way I could have admitted it to Jim and the others, but I had a problem with a knife. I knew I could defend myself in a fight with a knife if I had to, but I wasn't sure I could sneak up behind a man and kill him with one.

A plan was trying to form in my head where I might be able to get around one of those guards and put him out of the game some kind of way. If I could do that, I could get his gun and some ammunition. That's what I needed. But the images of how to go about it were bothering me. I couldn't help but shudder every time I thought of how it might feel to stab somebody.

By following the same path we had taken when we came across the grove of aspens, I got back over behind the little cabin. There was a big open space I'd have to cross to get close to the wall of the larger building. Lying still, I tried my best to hear the guard's footsteps as he walked up and down. I finally decided that if he was over there, he wasn't making a sound that I could hear. Finally, I got so tired of waiting I quit worrying about it and got myself ready to jump up and run.

Bending low to make less of a target in case anybody was looking my way, I ran across the open space. When I got beside the cabin wall I stood up straight and hugged it close, hoping no one would see me. I had to wait a few minutes to catch my breath and wait for my heart to stop pounding in my ears before I could start listening for the guard's footsteps again.

After a while I realized that nobody was guarding the cabin at all for some strange reason. I got up my nerve and worked along the wall to the front corner of the building. Still hugging the wall, I stopped to listen again. There was still no sound of anybody walking up and down. I stuck my head around the corner, thinking the guard might just be sitting or standing in front of the door. No one was there.

It was getting mighty dark, but I could see well enough in the weak moonlight to be sure that the only door to the cabin was padlocked shut, and there was no guard patrolling the building. More than likely that's because Blake and that Don person weren't nowhere around. All I could figure was the men that usually stood guard were taking themselves a holiday while their bosses were gone.

The problem I had to puzzle out was where the men who were supposed to be guarding the cabin might actually be. There simply had to be another cabin some place nearby. I vaguely remembered Jenny saying something about that earlier. It was back when my head was hurting me so bad. Did I hear her say the guards were in their cabin playing cards? I knew I was a little bit blurry about then, so I wasn't completely sure, but I vaguely remembered something being said about another cabin.

The moonlight was beginning to dim and the wind was getting up. It was beginning to make some noise in the pines. Soon it would be raining. The pale light marked the path heading into the trees. I was thankful for the coming storm. Without it the rising moon would soon make it so bright I'd be a sitting duck when I crossed open spaces.

I went around to the back corner of the big cabin. My thought was that I should try to listen for the sound of the guard's voices to find out where they were.

Suddenly I almost fell on my face. I stumbled into a huge pile of wood and brush that was stacked up against the back of the cabin. Shaken at my own clumsiness, I moved back into the shadow of the cabin wall and waited to see if anyone had heard me thrashing around.

The wind was beginning to make a lot of noise. The only sound I could hear over it was a sort of murmuring coming from the miners chained up inside the cabin. I reckon they mighta heard my footsteps while I was sneaking around the front of the cabin. They surely heard me almost falling down in that pile of sticks and leaves. They would be wondering who the heck I was and what I was up to.

Straining to see as the darkness increased, I couldn't spot any sign of anybody around. After a few minutes of not seeing or hearing any human sound, I figured I was safe. Ducking my head again, I ran for the short pines above the cabin.

A few steps along the narrow path I began to see a light flickering through the woods. It was only a couple of hundred yards up ahead of me. I knew it had to be those guards. They did have their own cabin. They were more than likely sitting up there passing the time by playing cards.

It's a wonder Blake hadn't set one of them to watching the cabin Jim and Will and me were locked in. I expect he might have ordered one of his men to watch that cabin. But if he did, that man plainly decided he'd rather play a little Poker or Three Card Monte or whatever he was doing in that cabin, instead of following orders and taking care of his boss' business.

It came to me then that riding with an outlaw gang can't be nothing like working for some rancher. I don't reckon men would feel the same about following orders. It probably ain't all that easy to fire members of a gang if they don't follow orders exactly right. It couldn't be easy to find new men to replace them either. It wasn't like you could talk it up around town or at the cattleman's association that you needed to hire a few new men.

Picking my way along through the woods, I got closer to the light that was shining out of the cabin window. I could hear men talking. Every once in a while there was a loud burst of laughter. It sounded like I was hearing more than two men talking. I finally worked myself up close enough to the cabin to see in the window. There were only two men in view, but it was clear to me after watching them for a few minutes that they were talking to at least one other man. Whoever it was sat far enough away from the window to where I couldn't see him. There were definitely at least three men in the cabin.

Well, of all the sorry luck, I thought.

Figuring out how to get the best of three men with no gun was a whole lot bigger mouthful than I had expected to bite off when I set out to do this stunt. I backed off from the cabin some and sat down on the ground trying to think of what to do. It come to me finally that maybe I could figure a way to split the men up so I could have a better chance at handling them.

After sitting there and chewing on it for a minute or two I finally got me a glimmering of an idea. I was feeling somewhat desperate by then I reckon, or I wouldn't have had the nerve to try what I did. I got up and walked real quiet-like over closer to the mine. I noticed earlier that they kept a little corral where they housed a couple of mules and some riding animals. That was before I got bashed on the head. So I was sincerely hoping I was remembering straight as I walked up the hill.

It wasn't long before I felt the top rail of a fence under my outstretched hand. I eased up close to the fence to look. The darkness was increasing now, and getting to be a problem, but I finally spotted the big brown mule they used to turn the contraption that pulverizes the big pieces of ore.

Turning back a few steps, I pulled a couple of hands full of grass from under my feet. Then I ducked under the fence and walked over to the mule. It didn't take long for me to make friends with him. I used both hands to rub on his ears and scratch up and down his nose. Most animals crave a little petting now and again. The poor old thing was probably ignored most of the time around here.

After a few minutes of rubbing his soft nose, I led the mule over to the corral gate and let him out. I turned back to shut the gate, then grabbed him by his halter to lead him up to the mine. By that time I'm thinking that mule would probably follow me any place I wanted him to go. I sincerely wished I could climb on his back and take off down the mountain.

Still holding on to his halter, I got the mule up close to the pole that turns the contraption the men were using to crush the ore. The harness was lying across the pole. I picked up the collar and hames and threw them across his shoulders. I was all the while cussing to myself because the harness had so much metal that it clinked together every move I made. After a while I got everything hooked up proper and settled the rest of the harness on the mule's back.

When I finally finished hooking him up to the pole I gave the mule a hard slap on his backsides and jumped to hide behind some rocks. I settled down about thirty yards away from the mule, well out of the way of the clearing and the path.

The timbers in the primitive crushing machine creaked and screeched as it started to turn. When it really got to moving the sounds settled down to that same deep rumbling, grinding noise I had heard the first time Will showed me this place. The mule ignored the noise like it wasn't even there. He kept on walking, turning the arrastrae around and around.

It wasn't even a minute after the noise started before I heard the door of the guards' cabin slam open. I peeped up over the rocks and saw the three men spill out of the door. The light from the lamp shone through the doorway. I couldn't recognize any of the men. They were moving too fast.

The guards disappeared in the darkness as they got away from the light. I kept still. I could hear them coming up the hill toward the mine. They were keeping under cover, and I'm sure they had their guns drawn. It was so dark I could barely see a shape move now and then. The men were staying pretty close together.

Finally, I spotted one of the men sneaking out of the shadows. I could see him fairly well from where I was hiding. He walked past me and eased slowly over beside the mule. He held his pistol in his right hand and kept sort of jerking around to look down the path behind him. He acted a lot like he was just plain scared. It wasn't long before he got close enough to the mule to put his hand on his harness. He caught ahold of something and held back hard. The animal stopped turning the machine.

As soon as the noise of the arrastrae stopped the man yelled back down to the others. "There's somebody sneaking around here playing tricks on us. This here mule didn't hook himself up to this pole."

I could hear the clink of metal against metal. The man was unbuckling and unhooking the mule's harness. He yelled again. "One of you men get yourself down to the little cabin and check on those other prisoners. I'm going to look around up here some more."

A voice called from the pines. "I'm going down and walk guard on the mine crew, like I'm supposed to be do-

ing, Bill. This might be a trick to try to get them men out
of there. Yell out if you need me."

Well, it worked. I had whittled the opposition down to
one person all right, but I still didn't know exactly how I
could get him out of the game without warning one or both
of the other two. I knew that whatever I did I couldn't make
any noise about it. I also had to make sure that guard didn't
yell or anything or the two other crooks would be after me.
I pulled the Bowie out of my belt and got ready to jump
the man when he walked by me with the mule.

I should have known I'd have to stop and start thinking
about stabbing the man. The other guard had called him
Bill. This really was a matter of life or death to me. I had
no doubts that this man or the people he was working with
would stab me if they had the chance. Heck, they'd probably enjoy it. But I suddenly knew it was impossible for
me to do it. *My conscience would never let me sneak up
on a man and cut his throat or just stab him in the back.
I had to find me some other way to stop him and shut him
up at the same time.*

In desperation I patted the ground near the boulders. After searching around for a second or two my hand closed
around a rock about half as big as a man's head. I put the
Bowie back in my belt and got myself ready to jump.

As the guard walked by me I stood up and reached out
to grab his collar in one hand. I jerked him backward with
that hand and slammed the rock down on the top of his
head with every ounce of strength I had in my other arm.
He made a sort of a gurgling sound down deep in his throat
and crumbled right down to the ground. I stepped back as
he fell and ran back to hide in the rocks in case one of
them other men mighta heard or seen what I was doing.

Listening for the sound of movement, I waited a few
minutes to make sure the man was really out. I think he
was out cold before he hit the ground. I went back over
and knelt beside him to make sure he was still alive. I

actually felt relieved that he was. That didn't stop me from taking his pistol and ammunition belt. The belt was full of extra shells. I knew I was surely going to need them before this night was over.

I untied the man's kerchief from around his neck and stuffed it in his mouth. Taking my mine off, I tied it around his head to hold the gag in place. I knew if I didn't shut him up good he'd be yelling as soon as he came back to himself.

I patted him down and found a leather riata tied on his belt, so I cut that in half and used it to tie his hands and feet. I pulled up on the tail ends of the rawhide hanging around his ankles and tied his feet and hands together behind his back.

The guard was still out cold when I left him. He was far enough from the main path to be fairly well-hidden, as dark as it was. I kept low so I'd be harder to see, and started to work my way downhill through the trees. I was thankful to feel a few drops of rain falling again. It was beginning to sound serious this time. The noise of the rain falling through the trees and hitting the ground would soon be enough to cover any noise I made.

After a few steps I heard someone calling out. It was the other guard—the one the guard named Bill had sent to check on the little cabin.

"Hey Bill," he yelled. "Them men that was locked up in that little cabin are long gone, even the crippled one. The cabin's empty. I couldn't see no light showing so I went on down to the main cabin. The door's standing wide open and that girl of Blake's is gone too. Come on down here."

When the guard called Bill didn't answer, the man called again. The continued silence apparently scared him. I could hear him talking in an agitated voice to the other guard as he got closer to the big cabin. I suddenly realized he was telling the guard to go ahead and fire the place like the Captain ordered.

I wondered for a minute what in the world he could be referring to when he said *fire the place*. Then I knew. I was horrified, but without a doubt, I was right. That pile of trash and wood I stumbled through behind the cabin was piled up there to provide fuel for a quick fire. Those men had been ordered to burn the cabin with the miners in it if there was trouble.

The other guard yelled, "You go saddle our horses, Benny. We're going around the mountain to get the heck out of here. First I'm gonna set this fire like Captain Blake said for us to if anybody ever found this place. We'll go on over to Colorado Springs to the old house and wait for Blake or we can just keep on riding. We'll talk and decide on that later."

I couldn't believe the evil. Just thinking about it made me shudder. They had planned all along to burn the cabin where the prisoners where chained. It was the way they had chosen to destroy any evidence if anybody happened to find out what they were doing.

To know that those two men were down there setting a match to the wood and leaves that was piled up against the back of the cabin seemed unreal. They had laid the fuel for the fire and had it ready and waiting for a situation like this.

The smell of smoke was already drifting up the hill. I cussed to myself as I waited impatiently to hear the sound of horses leaving so I could get down to the cabin without having to fight with those men. They seemed to be taking forever. I wanted to try to get those miners out of the cabin before the fire reached them.

As soon as I heard the sound of horses running off toward the aspens I jumped up and ran as fast as I could down the hill. I was panting when I rushed around to the front of the big cabin. The door was still padlocked. I started looking for something to use to force the door, then I remembered seeing a woodpile over behind Blake's cabin.

I ran around to the rear of the cabin and kicked the fire apart, hoping to slow it down, but the building was old, and built of heart pine logs. Several of them were already blazing. Flames were shooting up to the roof.

An axe was what I needed. Running down the hill like a madman I reached the woodpile and there it was. The axe was stuck upright in a log. I grabbed it and ran back up the hill and around to the front of the cabin.

The axe made short work of the padlock, but when I yanked the door open clouds of black smoke came pouring out. The smoke was so heavy that when it hit me in my face I thought I'd never be able to draw another breath. I could hear the trapped men crying and begging and praying.

I hoped that the keys for the blasted log chain would be hanging on a nail somewhere near the door. I patted along the wall trying to find them. There was no such luck.

I had to hurry. I could see enough through the smoke to spot the big iron ring driven into one of the logs to hold the end of the log chain. The trapped men were all crowded up as close to the front end of the platform as they could get to keep away from the fire, but the smoke was getting really bad. The men were coughing and wheezing. After about two breaths I was just as bad off.

Raising the axe up over my head I took a wild swing at the log where the iron ring held the end of the log chain. I cut a fair sized chunk of wood out, exposing the shaft of the ring, but it was still holding steady. Several of the men saw what I was doing and started pulling on the chain. I got myself set and chopped down on the log again as hard as I could.

The ring was loosening. I could hardly breathe. Lifting the axe I made one more swing. The men yanked the ring out of the wall. They frantically pulled on the loosened chain to get it out from between their ankles and out of their shackles. Some of the men almost fell out of the cabin

door. Others helped each other make their way out of the
smoke.

Still holding on to the axe I turned to run out and was
almost knocked flat by a big black man. He was supporting
an older man who was coughing so hard he was bent over
almost to the floor. As soon as I managed to get myself
close to the door and saw that all the men were up on their
feet, I dragged myself out of there, pulling a tall, thin man
along with me. He was coughing so much he could hardly
get along.

When we got far enough away to be safe from the fire
I turned to look back. The cabin was an inferno. I almost
hoped sparks from it would catch the whole camp on fire.
But the rain had started falling hard. The fire was burning
hot enough to consume the cabin, but it wouldn't spread.

The men flopped down on the ground gasping to get their
breath. I felt as bad off as they looked. I fell down beside
them and we all just lay there and watched the cabin burn.
I was feeling almighty thankful to be alive. After a few
minutes one of the men got on his feet to come over and
put his hand on my shoulder. His voice was hoarse from
coughing.

"God bless you son. We had given ourselves up for dead.
Those dirty, unnatural sons of something foul were going
to roast us alive."

I was still having a little trouble breathing myself. I swallowed a lot of smoke when I was working to get that chain
loose.

"Are all the men okay?" I asked between coughs.

"A couple of them are still coughing a lot. I think their
lungs may have been weak to start off with."

Another man kept looking around like he was trying to
see into the shadows left by the reflection of the fire.

"Are all of Blake's men gone?" he asked.

"I think they are, for the moment. Except for one of the
guards. The others called him Bill. He's tied up with his

own riata over near the mine. I heard the other two guards ride out of here just before I ran down and opened the cabin door."

"I see you're still holding on to that axe. Will you try to cut these chains in two so we can move a little easier?"

I felt sort of guilty for not thinking to offer to do that myself. The man shouldn't a even had to ask me.

"Let's go on down toward Blake's cabin. There's a big log at the woodpile out back. He's been using it for a chopping block. It'll probably make a handy place for us to cut these chains in two."

I noticed the big black man again when the men started to get to their feet—the same one that almost ran me down earlier. There was something about him that looked familiar. All of a sudden, I had me an idea.

I walked over beside the man and asked, "Would your name happen to be Davis?"

He gave me a hard look and drew back a little before he answered. "I'm Clement Davis. Why're you asking?"

I held out my hand. "I figured you might be. And I'm some kinda glad to meet up with you. I've got a young friend that goes by the name of Will Davis. That poor kid is walking around thinking his Pa has been dead for about a month, murdered at his diggings by some claim jumpers."

Davis reached out to grab my hand in his. His face was a study. "You know my boy? Will's all right? Where is he?"

"Hey now, slow yourself down." I said. I couldn't help laughing a little. I was thinking there was a few good things left in this world after all.

"Will's all right. He had sort of a hard time for a while, right after you disappeared, but he's come through fine. Blake and a couple of his cronies captured him yesterday and brought him up here, but he's free now. I've got a little mining claim and a camp set up down by the lake. Will was going to wait for me there, after he and my friends get some law to come up here and clean out this nest of crooks. Will's sort of been my helper in trying to get a friend of mine free from this mess."

"Thank you for telling me." Davis said. "I've been about crazy, worrying about all the things that could happen to that boy."

"Will's a fine youngster, Davis. You can rightly be proud of him. He'll be one happy boy when he finds out that you're alive, I sure know that."

The rain started to come down in earnest. It was probably a good thing. That meant that the fire would stop with the cabin. Those old pine logs made such a hot fire it could have burned off every tree on the mountain.

The entire group of men started walking down toward Blake's cabin. Their chains clanked with every step they took. The sound literally made my hair stand up on the back of my neck. It was truly scary to think of what I managed to escape.

About the time we reached the woodpile a tall miner came up close to me and said, "I was too busy coughing when we were back there in the light to speak to you, Kendrick. But I want to thank you. Lots of men would never have even tried to help us. I thought sure you'd run out from that cabin to save yourself when you couldn't put your hands on the keys to that log chain. Most people wouldn't have worried themselves none about a bunch of chained up strangers."

A shock went down my spine when I looked closer at the man. It took me a couple of seconds to recognize him. He was as tall as I am, but as dark as I am fair. He looked terrible. Even in the gloom he looked like he had been starved and mistreated for weeks.

I finally put a name to him. "It's Evan Williamson, the wheelwright, isn't it?

"It is for fair, Kendrick. What's left of me that is."

"Well, Evan, if I had thought of you at all I would have

pictured you working around your shop, maybe building somebody another wagon. Or maybe enjoying a drink down to Bell's saloon. Tell me what in the world happened. How did you ever get mixed up in this mess?"

"There ain't nothing new about it. I heard talk around the diggings about men going missing once they found a little gold, but I thought I could get through to Belden as long as I traveled in the day."

"I took off down the hill right in front of everybody. In fact, I went over to the mine office and went in and told that Blake girl I had sold my claim and was heading down the mountain. I thought it would make me safer if I made sure folks knew I was traveling, but I think I told the wrong somebody when I told her."

"I was near-about all the way down the hill when three yahoos with bandanas tied around their faces rode out of the pines right beside me. They fixed their rifles on me before I could blink. There was no way for me to get ahold of a gun to defend myself without getting killed. I figure that's the way they got most of these men."

"You're probably right about that."

"I found out later that the men that grabbed me were the same ones that worked as guards up here in Blake's mine. I remembered after a while seeing one of the men standing on the porch of the mine office when I went in there that day. The other two were strangers to me."

"Do you think the man that was on the porch heard you say you were leaving, or do you think Blake's girl told him about you?"

"Well, I don't know for sure, Kendrick. There ain't no way I could know that."

"What do you think?"

"The same as most of us think. I ain't got no proof, but I think the girl used some sort of signal to let those men know whenever some miner with a fair amount of dust left the mountain. They found some way to ride through the pines and get down the hill before we did so they could grab us.

"After the men braced me, they tied me on my horse and brought me up here along with my pack mule. They came about half the way on a path through the woods so's nobody around the diggings would see them.

"When we got here they went through my belongings and took everything I had, right there in front of me. They helped themselves to my money, my gold, and my extra clothes. They even took a likeness of my wife. They stood right there in front of me and argued over whose turn it was to get my clothes and other stuff."

"That's hard to believe." I shook my head in disgust. It was almost more than a regular person could accept as a real true thing to hear about men acting like that.

"Those men acted like robbing miners was a regular thing for them to do." Williamson went on, "Their actions made it plumb clear to me that they had no intention of ever letting me leave out of this place alive, either."

"It's hard to understand men like Blake and his crew, ain't it?" I said, wondering to myself if Jenny was a straight shooter or if she really had been helping Blake rob and capture the miners all along.

"They're sure hard men, that's a fact." Williamson said.

I heard the sound of the axe. Davis was using it to cut the chains in two on each man's leg and wrist irons. I walked over closer to see how he was doing it. The men draped their chains over the piece of log they were using as a chopping block and Davis gave a mighty swing of the axe. Every time it hit the block the force of the blade would shear a link in half, breaking the chains.

Several of the men were over near the cabin swinging their arms around and lifting their legs up and down. It looked like they were sort of testing them to see if they still worked right. Hanging loose like that, their chains were making more noise than ever.

There was sort of a tickling between my shoulder blades. It was the second time I felt it. I was beginning to feel kind of jittery standing around. I knew Blake and his sidekick would be on their way up the mountain sometime before the night was over. I didn't know how much time had passed since they had left the mine, but even though it was raining hard they were almost bound to see the cabin burning if they came up the road any time soon. I wondered if they would still come back up here when they saw the fire or what they might end up doing.

Then I thought, *shucks, of course they'll come back here. Blake's got gold hid up here somewhere. He'll never ride off and leave that.*

I knew it was time I did something about the guard I left tied up near the mine. Then I'd needed to figure out how to get these men out of this place. I finally decided that maybe the best thing for me and the men to do would be to hide ourselves in the woods.

I was armed with the pistol I took off of the guard and had a few extra shells for it, but the rest of the men were unarmed. I knew I wouldn't be able to hold off Blake and the other man with no more firepower than that. They would surely have rifles in addition to their handguns.

But wait a minute, I thought. I remembered that just as they were leaving Jenny had been saying something to Jim about the guns that were taken from the men Blake captured.

I walked over to the group of men whose chains were cut. "Let's go search Blake's cabin. I think I heard his stepdaughter say he had a trunk in there that's chock-a-block full of pistols and long guns that he and his men took offa the miners. It's a pretty sure thing that Blake and his sidekick will be coming back up here tonight and I'd feel a whole lot better if more of us were armed."

There was a chorus of agreement to that, and I followed several of the men around to the front of the cabin. The door was standing wide open, and we walked right in. I lit a match. Holding it high, I found the lamp sitting on the table. It was hard to imagine that only three nights earlier I had seen the light from that lamp shining out of the door as Jenny peacefully washed dishes. I dug out another match, lit the lamp, and held it up so we could see around the whole room.

The room looked clean and neat, if small. The only furnishings in the place besides the table with benches on each side were two built-in bunks on the left wall, and a large wooden trunk. I sure hoped it was the one with the guns.

Rough shelves loaded with supplies were nailed up on the wall behind the table, and there was an iron cook stove. Over in the back corner of the room a ladder went up to an opening in the ceiling. I figured it led to a sleeping loft. That was probably where Jenny slept.

Two of the men made straight for the big trunk and started beating on the lock to get it open, but a couple of the others went over to the shelves near the cook stove to examine the tins and boxes of food.

Evan Williamson came in the cabin to stand beside me. I caught his eye and jerked my head toward the men who were pulling cans of food down off the shelves and piling them up on the table.

He laughed a little when he saw where I was looking and said, "Don't be surprised none by that. Ain't none of us had a awful lot to eat lately considering how hard we've been working. I don't know if Blake and them were running low on supplies or if they were just mean. They mighta thought to keep us hungry just out of pure meanness, it wouldn't surprise me none."

Walking over to the men who were taking the food off the shelves, I asked, "Will a couple of you men cook up some food for everybody?"

One of the miners nodded, but I couldn't hear them answer. There was too much noise. One of the men standing over beside the trunk was waving a bunch of keys up over top his head and yelling at the top of his lungs. He had unlocked the bracelets that were around his wrists and was holding them up in his other hand. The hubbub those men made when they realized that man was holding the keys to unlock the iron bracelets around their wrists and ankles was out and out deafening.

When all eight of the men got their irons unlocked and things began to calm down again, I noticed that one of the men had the cook stove stoked up and two pans of bacon were sizzling. Another man was up to his elbows in a dishpan, mixing biscuit dough. I could smell coffee boiling.

While the food was cooking I helped dole out guns from the trunk. There were plenty for every single one of the men to have a handgun and a rifle or shotgun. I wondered how many men the guns represented. If the number of guns was any indication, it had to be a whole lot more than the few standing there in front of me. I claimed my own rifle and handgun when I found them.

I noticed that several of the men were crowded around something over near the door. When I got closer I saw that they had a dishpan full of water and a pile of rags. They were taking turns washing their hands and faces and cleaning the scrapes and sore places left on their wrists by the shackles. It wasn't long before everybody finished washing up and got a plate or pan piled high with food. The men sat down on the floor or anywhere they could to eat.

The food smelled wonderful, and I ate with the best of them. I couldn't help watching as different ones finished eating and jumped up to hurry outside in the rain. When I finished eating I thanked the men who cooked the food and headed outside to see what the men were doing.

Davis and two others were over by the edge of the aspens. They seemed to enjoy standing out there with the rain running down their faces. Each man carried a long gun over his arm. I think the men were hoping Blake would ride in so they could get a chance at him.

I started to walk over to talk to Davis. I got a little tickled as I got close to him. From the way he was acting, he was probably just about as doggoned bossy as that boy of his was.

Davis moved away from the other men to stand close so I could hear him. "I think we should send two men up to the mine and two more to stand guard over near the corral. There's different ways into this canyon and we don't want anybody to sneak up on us. I don't know if there's any riding horses left up here or not, but come daylight, we need to find out. There were two horses in the corral earlier, but they're the ones the guards took. Aside from the mules they used to run that rock crusher I don't think there's any more animals.

"Don't let's send anybody up that way yet, Davis. You and I need to go first and figure out what we should do with that guard I tied up."

"Which one of the guards is it?"

"Be blessed if I know for sure. All I can tell you is he was at least a foot shorter than me and kind of dark skinned. That's all I know. I ain't sure, but I think I might have heard one of the other guards calling him Bill."

"That sounds some like that snake that carried the Greener all the time. There's a road beyond that bunch of aspens there that winds around that pile of rocks. I got a pretty good look at it when they brought me up here. It's not much more than a path cut back in the rocks. I remember I thought at the time it didn't look wide enough for a wagon.

"There's a deep arroyo that runs along one side of the road. I've not been close to it, but I would guess it's a hundred feet deep or more. I know for a fact there's at least three bodies down there. We saw them drag one poor man off and throw him down there and I heard the guards talking about the other two."

"My friend told me he heard about what happened to that poor man. Jim said he heard him scream after they shot him."

"Blake and his men have got themselves another cabin and corrals around that track somewhere." Davis continued. "I don't think it's very far. I heard them talking about it. They've got a man that stays there and keeps some horses ready in case the gang needs to make a getaway."

"Let's go on up the hill and check on that guy I tied up. We can bring him down and lock him in the little cabin. I don't think we have to worry any if Blake comes back up here right now. He'll be up against an army."

"That he will. And every man jack of this army feels exactly the same way I do after being chained up like that. They want his sorry scalp for a keepsake."

Chapter Nine

Davis followed me as we walked along the narrow path toward the mine. I could see the guard's light colored shirt a fair distance before we reached him. The man was awake and watched us approach. When we got up close enough to see his face Davis struck a match so he could identify the man. I thought the guard's eyes looked a little bit scared like. Maybe it was seeing Davis standing there with no chains. He was right to be scared, that's a fact. I glanced up when the light from the match hit Davis' face. He didn't look at all friendly.

I took out the bowie and cut through the rawhide rope that held the man's arms and legs together behind his back. He groaned as he stretched his legs out straight. I reckon he had been a mite uncomfortable with his legs pulled back behind him thataway. I sort of hoped he was.

I nodded to Davis and we both reached down to take hold of the man under his arms and lift him upright. He was a little unsteady as he tried to stand up. His legs had probably gone to sleep from staying in such an awkward position for so long. I used the knife to remove the rest of the riata from his ankles while Davis held him up by one arm, then I took the gag out of his mouth.

He sputtered a few times. I expect his mouth felt like it was full of cotton. He didn't say a word though, he just kept watching every move Davis made.

"Let's go," I said.

Me and Davis took the man's arms again and sort of led him and sometimes dragged him down the hill. I hoped none of the other miners would see us before we got him locked in the cabin. I didn't think they could be trusted not to try to tear him apart. I felt sure I wouldn't be able to stop them. I sneaked a couple of looks over at Davis' face. It was easy to see that he wasn't any too calm about it himself.

Davis held on to the man while I got the cabin door open. I struck a match and held it up high, looking for the lantern Jenny left when she let us out of the cabin. I found it, but my match went out and I had to dig around in my pocket to find another one to get the thing lit.

While I was fiddling with the light Davis guided the man over to stand beside the same cot I was tied up on. When I held the lantern up high I saw Davis put one of his big fists in the middle of the outlaw's chest and shove him down to a sitting position. The push was definitely a little harder than necessary.

"Hey, what are you going to do with me?" The man asked. The light revealed the fear on his face.

"We haven't decided yet." Davis answered before I could say anything. "We've been thinking about giving you to your former prisoners," he continued with a nasty looking grin.

I allowed to myself that I better start talking, fast. Davis probably was only acting tough, but I wanted to question the man about the hideout around the other side of the rocks and a few other things, not watch Davis and the other miners tear him into little pieces.

"What's your name?" I asked.

"I'm Bill Gamble. Who the devil are you?"

"My name's Kendrick. I was captured by Blake and locked up in this cabin with two other men until we escaped earlier tonight."

"How in the devil did you ever get out of here?"

"Blake's daughter opened the door and helped us get away. I decided to come back and break up your party."

"That sorry, stuck-up little double-dealing traitor." Gamble's face contorted with anger.

"Easy now, I'll have to take exception if you say anything against that young lady after she let me out of this hole."

"If that lowdown little sneak helped you get out of here she did it for a reason. You can bet on that. That woman's been in on everything that ever went on up here. She thought up a lot of the things Blake's done. I know for a fact she's worked with Blake for a long time. She's been at it at least as long as I've known him, and that's been more than ten year."

"She's a lot older than she looks too. Nobody loves a dollar like that there woman does. I'd bet you even money that wench took a big chunk of the money and gold Blake had stashed when she left here."

Davis interrupted, "Shut up about the woman. We don't care. Tell us about the hideout outside the canyon and where Blake hides the gold from the mine. If you help us we might think about letting you live."

"I ain't telling you anything."

Davis' face sort of closed up, but he didn't say a word. He reached over and picked up Gamble's feet and swung him around so his legs were up on the cot. He wasn't being any too gentle about it either. Gamble must of felt awful to be handled like that when he was helpless. I know I would have. Davis leaned over to pick up a couple of the short pieces of rope that were lying on the floor and used them to tie the man's feet to the frame of the bunk.

When he got Gamble's feet secured, Davis loosened the rope that held his hands behind his back and pushed him to a prone position on the cot. Then he re-tied his hands to the other end of the cot.

"There, you lowdown piece of dirt. You're going to stay right there until you decide to help us or we get tired of talking and turn you over to the rest of the miners. All I have to do is call out. They're right down at the bottom of the hill."

"Easy Davis," I said.

"There's no easy about it. This is one of those sorry stinking snakes that's been holding a gun on me and making me pound rocks for more'n a month. I saw the sick animal laughing out loud two or three different times when he saw that crazy brute Don beating on us men with that whip he carries around."

"Wasn't nothing I could do to stop that" Gamble said.

"You could have quit such a lowdown job and left."

"Calm yourself now, Davis," I said. "There's no need to argue with the man. You go on outside and guard the door so none of the other miners can get in. Let me talk to him."

Davis deferred to me, but the way he moved he made it obvious he didn't want to. I felt relieved when he did. I wasn't completely sure he would cooperate at all until he started moving. He stepped back away from Gamble and walked over to stand beside the door with his arms crossed.

I nodded toward the door. "Please go outside."

He gave me a hard look, like he might want to tell me to go some place hot my own self, but he went out, slamming the door hard enough to almost knock it off its hinges.

"Well, Bill," I said. I squatted down beside the cot to talk to him. "It looks like you better talk to me. I'm down right put out at you and all of Blake's crew, but I won't tear you apart or hang you, and I'm afraid that's what Davis and the rest of those men want to do."

"You can't give me to them miners, they're crazy."

"Don't kid yourself that I won't do exactly that if you don't talk."

"If you do you're as bad as Blake ever was."

"Now you're beginning to make me mad."

I got up and went over to the door. Grabbing the handle with my left hand I turned to face Gamble. "Give me one good reason why I shouldn't just let Davis do what he wants?"

"Come back, mister, please. I'll tell you anything you want to know."

Gamble strained to hold his head up as high as he could. Light from the lantern was shining on beads of sweat standing out on his forehead.

"Are you really ready to talk to me?" I asked.

"I swear I am."

"I don't have time to fool with you if you're lying."

"Just ask me, I'll tell you anything you want to know."

"Okay then."

I walked back over close to the cot and looked down at Gamble. "Tell me what's at the other end of that side road that goes around the rock wall and how many of Blake's men are waiting around there."

"It's a ranch. There's usually only one man over there. His name is Jed Millerschmidt. He's one of Blake's old gang who got crippled up in a bank robbery that went bad a couple of years back. He tends the stock and keeps care of the place. Blake sets a heap of store by him."

"How crippled up is this Millersmith?"

"It's Millerschmidt. He gets real fussy about people saying his name right, and he can still use a pistol."

"Blast him and his pistol. What I want to know is how well he can get around."

"He can still get around all right, but he's got a gimp leg and only one arm. His left arm was shot up so bad it had to be took off just above the elbow."

"Do you think he would have left with the other two men?"

"I think so. I know I woulda." Gamble's eyes looked funny and he looked away when he said it. I figured he was lying about that.

"Where does the road come out?" I asked.

"Right beside the barn."

I walked over and opened the door. Davis was standing close.

"Did you hear everything he said?"

He nodded without answering.

"We should go over there."

"I don't know about that. What can we do about the other miners? I know how I feel about this pig. The rest of them probably feel worse than I do." Davis' face looked stiff and his hands were fists.

"If we leave Gamble here alone and they find out he's here, they'll break the door down and probably beat this bum to death."

"I've got a little cash money, do you think they would take it and walk down to Belden?"

"I don't know if they would or not. I know most of them are mighty anxious to get word to their folks that they're all right, but they want a piece of Blake and that Don fella pretty doggoned bad."

"Blake might come back here in the next few minutes or it might be sometime during the day tomorrow before he gets here. He mighta decided to stay in town overnight because of the rain. The storm could have been worse down there on the flat." I was sort of talking to myself and to Davis at the same time.

"Let's go talk to those men. If they'll take an Eagle or two apiece and go on down the mountain it would be the best thing all around, I'm thinking. Do you reckon they'll trust me if I promise to bring all the money or gold I find up here to the sheriff's office in Belden so they can get their stuff back?"

"Considering their behinds would be burnt to a crisp right now if it weren't for you, they shouldn't have any trouble trusting you about money."

I rechecked the combination of rawhide and ropes holding Gamble to the cot. He looked secure. I led the way out and shoved a stick through the loop to hold the door shut. I took the padlock and threw it as far as I could.

"Why'd you do that?" Davis asked.

"If any of those men come up here and see this door padlocked they're sure to think it's hiding something valuable of Blake's and force the door open to find out what it is."

"Well kiss my foot. I'd a never thought of that in a million years."

Davis and I walked down the hill to join the group of men standing around in front of the other cabin. I hoped Evan Williamson would agree to stay here and help us try to capture Blake and his sidekick, but I knew the men were bound to be anxious to leave.

I was convinced that some of the miners would take off pretty quick no matter what I said. In fact, I was kinda surprised to see that none of them had disappeared while Davis and me moved the guard. It did seem to me like it would be a whole lot better for them if they would leave here as a group.

Stepping back a step or two I spoke out fairly loud, "Men, I know Blake and his crooks robbed you of everything you owned. I also know that most of you have family you want to contact as soon as possible. I've got a proposition for you. I've got enough money in my pocket to give each of you twenty dollars. I want you to take it and walk down to Belden. The town has a telegraph if you need it so you can let your family know you're all right, and you'll have a chance to get cleaned up and buy yourselves some decent clothes."

"I'm asking Clement Davis here and Evan Williamson to stay and help me capture Blake and the rest of his gang. We'll also try to find out where he's hidden the money he stole from you men and the gold you helped dig out of the mine here."

"Why shouldn't we stay here and help you capture Blake?" one of the miner's asked.

I turned to face him before I spoke. The men were quiet. I asked him straight out, "Would you try to capture him?"

The whole group started to talk at once. Several yelled how they would "carve out his liver and lights," and commit various other vicious and unlawful acts if they ever got their hands on Blake or that guard named Don.

"That's exactly what I'm worried about." I said.

"We need to take Blake alive if we can. He's probably the only one who knows exactly where all the money and gold is hidden. If you men stay here and draw down on Blake and his sidekick with all this firepower, they'll naturally shoot back and somebody's going to end up dead."

"With the kind of luck that's been going around here lately that might be you or me. It'll surely be Blake and his sidekick. If Blake's killed before we find out where he keeps the gold and the money he stole, I don't see any hope of you men ever getting your money back."

The men began talking among themselves. I was certain I'd gotten to them with the idea of maybe getting back some of their belongings.

"How would we ever get any of our money back anyway?" A short miner with a white beard asked. His voice sounded hard and bitter.

"Don't the law keep the loot they take from outlaws?"

"I'll give you my word, men. You give Williamson here your name and direction before you leave. Take a guess at the value of what Blake and his men took from you when they captured you and he'll put that down too. I'll personally see that whatever money we find here or in Blake's possession will be used to pay you men back as far as it will go. I'll go to the governor to make it happen if I have to."

Davis stepped around beside me, facing the group of men.

"I'm downright ashamed to say this, but you men need to be reminded of something. Kendrick here saved our lives tonight. We'd have been roasted alive right now if it wasn't for him. Go ahead and do like he's asking you to do. You know you can trust him."

That seemed to take care of any argument against my plan. Davis and I led the group inside the cabin so we could find something to write their names on. Davis scrambled around and found a piece of wrapping paper on a shelf, and using the stub of a pencil from my shirt pocket, Williamson sat down at the table ready to write down each man's information.

Before I passed out the money to the men I said, "You men wait for me in Belden. I'd be obliged if the first thing you do when you get there is go to Sheriff Dillard's office and find out if Jim Cason arrived there all right. Either way, get the sheriff to send us some help up here as fast as possible."

I shut up then and passed out the twenty-dollar gold pieces. Each of the men took time enough to shake my hand and thank me for getting them loose from that chain and saving them from burning up.

By the time we finished getting all the information from the last miner, the rest of them had left the cabin and melted away into the trees. I didn't even get a chance to remind them to stay clear of the road until they reached town. I guess they'd learned that lesson, though—the hard way.

Davis gave me the piece of paper with the names of the men. I noticed that none of them claimed to have lost more than a thousand dollars. Most of them listed amounts nearer to five hundred. That was still a lot of money. Enough to set a man and his family set up in a business or to buy and stock a decent farm.

I was pretty certain that a lot of the men Blake captured hadn't made it. Their bodies were probably in the bottom of that arroyo if they died up here at the mine. If they were killed at the time of the robbery their remains were most-likely rotting in the woods somewhere near the road to Belden.

Blake had to have several thousand dollars squirreled away somewhere. What with all the money and gold his men stole from the miners, plus the gold the kidnapped men dug out of Jim's mine.

"Let's douse the light and get the heck out of here, Davis." I said. "I want to check out Blake's hideout around the other side of those rocks. If we hang around here much longer we're liable to get caught in a shooting war."

Davis leaned over and blew out the lamp. As we stepped outside I noticed that rain still dripped from the cabin roof, but the sky was beginning to clear. I shut the door to the cabin as we left. The path was hard to see until our eyes got used to the gloom, but we made it back up the hill to the little cabin.

Remembering how badly it shook me when Blake's men yanked the door open and made a lot of noise when I was tied up in that shed made it seem like a good idea for me to shake Gamble up the same way if I could. It might help make him talk some more. I pounded on the door with my fist, then yanked it open and stomped on the floor as hard as I could.

"Who is that? Get away. Get away from me." Gamble literally screamed.

"It's Kendrick. I've come to give you a final chance to help us. Tell us where Blake keeps his gold and the loot you men stole from the miners."

I was standing right up close beside the cot by that time—almost yelling down in Gamble's face.

"I don't know where he keeps anything," Gamble was almost sobbing. "I swear to God I don't. All I know is the gold is hidden somewhere near here. I never saw him take it around to the ranch. He always took the bags of dust inside his cabin. I swear, that's all I know."

"You better be telling me straight. There's a man here name of Clement Davis that's been begging me to let him stand guard over you for the rest of the night. You know the man I mean. If I thought you were lying I might go ahead and let him do that job."

"Mister, Davis will kill me. You can't mean to do that."

"Why shouldn't I?"

"It wouldn't be right. You've got me helpless."

"Shut up Gamble." The weasel was about to make me mad enough to give him to Davis with my blessing.

"I heard you talking to your buddies when you came up to the mine before the fire. You agreed with them to murder those men by burning them alive while they were chained down inside that cabin. You deserve anything you get."

I turned away then. Being in the same room with the man was making me feel mean.

I put the peg back in the door and motioned for Williamson and Davis to follow me. We walked across the open area north of the aspens and started downhill. I stayed in the edge of the road, but close against the rocks. I figured the shadows of the rocks would help to hide us if Blake happened along. I also knew it would be easier for me to find where the road forked to head around the rocks if I kept reaching my left hand out and touching the wall every now and then.

It wasn't long until we reached the spot where the other road curved around to the west. I kept on reaching out and touching the rocks with one hand. The base of the road felt like solid rock under my feet. All that rain had made the footing feel awful slick. I didn't want any of us to end up in the bottom of that arroyo by accident.

The rain had stopped completely and stars began to peep out. It looked like we might have enough light by the time we got to Blake's hideout to help us find that Smith whatever his name is without getting ourselves shot. It was way too much to hope for that we could take that place over without any shooting. I knew that.

My plan was to get to Blake's hideout and kill or capture any of his men that might still be there. It would help a lot if we could do that before Blake and his pal Don got back to the mine. The way I figured it, when Blake realized that all his men were gone and saw that the miner's cabin was burned to the ground, he'd grab his gold and rush around this road to the other hideout.

Of course it was always possible he had fetched his gold and other things over here and hid them long ago. That Gamble couldn't know everything.

If we could clear out that Smith or any other men that might be at the hideout before Blake got there we might be able to capture him alive. Then we'd be able to get our hands on the money and gold he stole from the miners.

I didn't think any of us would have a problem shooting Blake or his sidekick if it come to that. Still, I didn't hold out much hope for getting Blake alive. It was a pretty sure bet that he and his men would put up a hard fight.

We followed the twists and turns of the narrow track for more'n a quarter mile until we finally turned a corner and the barn loomed up. The building was almost black against the pale moonlight. It was big and a little bit scary-looking. All three of us felt compelled to sort of tiptoe as we walked alongside it for some reason. I know I did, and when I glanced around at Davis and Williamson they were copying me.

When I got close to the front corner of the barn I felt the edge of a doorframe. Fumbling around it until I got my hand on the door handle, I drew my gun and pushed the door open, careful to keep back in the shadows. After I studied a few seconds my eyes got adjusted to the gloom and I could see enough to decide the barn was empty.

Swinging the door wide open to get as much light as possible, I motioned for Davis and Williamson to follow me inside. We eased along past the stalls until we came to a door at the other end of the aisle. It was really dark inside the barn and hard to see. Everything was quiet. I motioned for Williamson to check the tack room. No horses stood in the stalls. Slowly easing one of the big double doors open a crack, I watched for any movement near the barn.

No light showed in the cabin, but I knew that didn't mean much. I was afraid to trust that all of Blake's men were gone. That Smith fella that looked after the place had been warned that something was up when those two guards who escaped from the mine came through here. He was more likely than not hiding somewhere, with his guns ready, watching for some fool like me to come sashaying around that barn.

There was a fresh breeze blowing, but the storm was completely over and the sky was clear. I could smell cattle somewhere close by. It was light enough for me to see a group of horses standing on the far side of the corral.

Seeing the horses cinched it for me. Blake's man was here somewhere. That was sure. He was probably sitting in the shack over beyond the corral with his gun ready. Just watching and waiting for us to step out of this barn.

"Hold it, men." I whispered to Davis and Williamson.

"We've got to get closer to the cabin, but find something to get behind quick. That caretaker is bound to be waiting around here someplace. I've got my doubts about it, but it's possible that the other two guards are here too."

Williamson wasn't quick enough. He ran out of the barn door and jumped for cover behind the corner of the corral, but I heard a thump as he hit the ground and the sound of a pistol shot at the same time.

"Evan, are you all right?" I asked, keeping my voice low.

I was lying flat in the yard by then, about thirty feet outside the barn door, but my only protection was a little rise in the ground. I didn't want that crook in the shack getting a bead on me by hearing my voice.

"I'm fine, Kendrick."

"Where're you hit, man?"

"I've got a burn on my arm, is all. It ain't hardly even bleeding. Don't worry none about me."

"The shooter's inside the shack."

"Hey Kendrick, think one of us can get close enough to set that shack on fire?" Davis asked in a loud voice.

He was over to my right, hiding behind a little building. It looked like either a smokehouse or a tool shed. About the time he finished speaking a barrage of shots came pouring out of the shack. This time the skunk was using a repeating rifle.

I could see well enough to spot Davis. He was lying down flat, but he was under cover and shooting back at the man. Holding my gun up over my head so I wouldn't gouge it down in the dirt, I rolled toward the corral. I wanted to know exactly how bad Williamson's wound was.

I rolled a couple of more times, and when I finally reached the corner post of the corral I got up on my knees beside Williamson.

"Are you all right?" I asked again. I could see a cut in his shirt on his upper left arm, but only a little blood was showing.

"You bet I am."

"That's bound to hurt."

"Forget about it. What are you going to do?"

"I'm going to work around to the other side of the corral and get closer to the shack."

"Be careful."

Without answering, I slid through the bottom two poles of the corral fence. Keeping my head low, I moved over so the horses were between me and the man firing the rifle. Talking real soft I patted the horses some as I passed so they'd stand still for me to work my way between them. When I reached the other side of the corral I climbed through the bars again and ran along outside the fence until I reached the corner closest to the cabin.

The man inside the cabin was still firing his rifle in Davis's direction. It looked like he hadn't even noticed me. Hoping he would keep it up for a few more seconds, I steadied my pistol on top the post at the corner of the corral. Aiming at the rifle's muzzle flash I emptied my gun into the window.

When I stopped firing my ears were ringing so hard I couldn't hear a doggoned thing. But I saw the man's rifle fall from the sill and land on the ground under the window.

"All's clear men," I yelled.

I could hear Williamson walking along the other side of the corral in the direction of the cabin. I heard Davis's footsteps when he joined him. I walked up close to the side of the cabin and picked up the man's rifle.

"I'll go on inside and make sure that ranny's dead." Davis said as he walked past me to step in the cabin door.

"Thanks. I sure ain't looking forward to it none, but I reckon I should go in with you."

"Shucks man, you didn't have no choice." Williamson was calm. "That jasper was purely out to kill us all."

"I know," I said.

"We've got to check this place and get ourselves set for Blake." I said over my shoulder to Williamson as I stepped in the cabin behind Davis. "He's gonna be coming along that road soon, and we've gotta be ready."

The cabin was trashed. In the glow of the match I held over my head we could easily see there was no woman around to keep the place decent. A few pans and dishes were sitting in a dry sink with food dried on them. Clothes and saddles and bottles were scattered everywhere.

Davis went over and lit another match to look the dead man over.

"The shooter was the man with one arm, that Millersmith." He said, as we left the cabin. "Here's his other rifle and a handgun."

"That's how he was able to throw so much lead so fast." Williamson said. "He loaded up all his guns and was sitting in that window waiting for us."

"Let's get all the weapons. Make sure they're loaded," I said.

"I'll take the extra pistol. I can stick it in my belt. This'll give each of you men two long guns and a pistol and I've got my rifle. We ought to be able to hold off a small army."

We talked it over and decided to hide in nearly the same places we had been earlier. I was on the backside of the corral and Williamson was on the side closer to the barn. Davis was hunkered down behind the small shed. We were positioned almost exactly like we were before except we were turned around facing the opposite way.

Chapter Ten

As it happened, we didn't have long to wait. I guess we were in position something less than an hour. We didn't hear a thing until a tall man stepped around the corner of the barn leading his horse. I figured him to be Blake. He had a heavy beard and wore the same black duster I saw the man in the cabin wearing that first time I went in the canyon.

I noticed that the man's horse moved like it was packing a heavy load. The big man called Don followed close behind the tall man's horse, and then came Gamble—the guard me and Davis had left tied up in the small cabin.

Gamble was leading another horse and Don was leading the same mule I had hooked up to the rock crusher. All three of the animals were loaded down with canvas bags. I knew it had to be the gold. The brazen devils.

Davis and Williamson were closest to the group of men but we had agreed that I would give the men a fair chance to surrender before we started shooting. I stood up where I was and fired in the air.

"Hold it where you are Blake. We're holding rifles on you men so don't make a move. Get your hands up in the air."

All three of the men ignored me and grabbed for their pistols. That was exactly what I expected to happen. I wasn't even needed. Davis and Williamson both fired four or five times in succession. By the time I got around the corral and down to where Williamson was standing, Blake and the other men were down on the ground shot to doll rags.

"You men don't believe in leaving anything to chance do you?"

Williamson almost growled. "They still didn't get punished nothing like they deserve."

"It mighta helped a little bit if we coulda taken at least one of them alive."

"They won't gonna be took alive, Kendrick. You seen that," Williams said.

Davis walked over to prod the men with the muzzle of his rifle to make sure they were dead. "Did you notice? These animals are loaded way too heavy. Let's redistribute these bags of gold onto three more of them horses in the corral. Then let's get ourselves down offa this mountain."

"Now you're talking." I said. "There's enough mounts here for each of us to have a horse to ride and two pack animals to lead."

I turned to Williamson and asked, "Is your arm all right for you to ride?"

"Don't you worry none about me son. I'll be there. Same as you."

We found packsaddles in the barn to put on three of the horses. Davis and I selected the sturdiest mounts for hauling the gold and shifted about half of the bags from the two horses and mule over to them.

While Davis and I were moving the gold and saddling a horse for each of us to ride, Williamson decided to search the three dead men.

"Here's a big bunch of notes drawn on the bank in Denver. They were stuffed down in the pockets of Blake's coat.''

''I'll bet that's the ten thousand dollar ransom Major Cason was to pay Blake for the release of his son. He'll be mighty grateful when you return it to him, Evan. I figure most folks would give you a big reward, but I'm not altogether sure what Cason will do, he's sort of chancy.''

''There's something else.''

''What?''

''That fella wearing Blake's coat ain't Blake.''

''What are you telling me?''

''It's pretty simple. The man we took to be Blake is somebody else. I ain't ever seen him before.''

''Let me see him,'' Davis said. Leaving the horses he was saddling, he came over and knelt beside the body of the tall man.

''I'll be blessed if you ain't right, Williamson. This sure ain't Blake.''

''What do you suppose happened?'' I asked.

''It's a mystery to me, but we better be careful.''

''Wait a minute now,'' I said. ''If that ain't Blake, then how come he's carrying the ransom money Blake went down to Cason's to collect?''

''That's a good question.'' Williamson said, scratching the side of his head in puzzlement.

''I've got an idea,'' Davis said, ''that maybe these fellas turned on Blake and killed him for the money and the gold.''

''You may be right about that,'' I said, ''but we better be darn careful until we find his body. We wouldn't want to run into him on the way out of here.''

''Let's go back over to the mine and search.'' Williamson said. ''These men probably killed Blake over there while he was packing up the gold. We wouldn't a never heard any shooting from the other side of them rocks.''

Each of us led two horses around the barn and along the

narrow road between the rocks and the arroyo. I went in front and tried not to think about falling over that drop into the arroyo. It had lightened up some more, but the shadows in that ditch made it look bottomless. When we were almost to the other side. I held up my hand for Davis and Williamson to stop.

"Get your guns ready. Blake or more of his crooks might be around the mine buildings."

"We're ready." Davis said.

I chuckled at that. I knew he was ready.

When we reached the mine road we turned our horses uphill and rode around the aspens to the mine buildings. At first everything seemed deserted. We tied the horses to some trees close to the main cabin. Williamson stayed with the horses while Davis and I walked around to check on things.

Nothing seemed out of place. When we got up close to the small cabin, I noticed that the little stick of wood used to hold the door tight looked new. That seemed sorta strange to me. *Why in the world would those outlaws close the door so careful like?* I wondered. *Was something important in there?*

We were almost up to the door when we heard a thump and the sound of groaning coming from inside the cabin. I looked over at Davis. He cocked his rifle as he pulled the stick out of the lock. We shoved the door all the way open and jumped back to the side in case somebody tried to shoot at us.

A man was half-lying, half-sitting on the floor beside the bunk. There was blood all over his right shoulder and side.

Davis pushed past me to walk over and nudge the man with his foot.

"Wake up, Blake." His words sounded like a growl.

The man roused himself and stared up at Davis.

"Water."

"You don't deserve water, you dirty murderer."

Squatting down beside Blake I pulled his shirt aside trying to see exactly where and how badly he was wounded.

"Go get my canteen, Davis."

"The devil I will."

"Please go get my canteen? We can take this man down to Belden with us if he's not wounded too badly and hold a trial. We might even find out how many men he's killed. Wouldn't you be satisfied to see him hang?"

"No, Kendrick, I don't think I would be satisfied, it just ain't enough. I know he's too bad off for me to be hitting or shooting on him. It just galls me."

He turned away, then said, "Don't fret yourself, I'll go get the water."

Blake was more aware than I thought. As soon as Davis went out of the room he whispered. "My men took my gold and shot me. They knew I was alive, but left me here to die."

"That makes no difference now, Blake. We'll get you some water and tie your side up so it won't start bleeding again. You're going to have to ride down to Belden to get to a doctor."

"I'll die if you make me ride like this."

"No you won't. You might be hurting bad enough to think so, but you won't die from this. It looks like you've lost a lot of blood, but I think if I tie your side up good and tight it won't start up bleeding again, even with you bouncing around on the back of a horse for a couple of hours."

"I can't stand the pain." Blake said.

He closed his eyes and let his head fall back against the side of the bunk. I couldn't tell if he had fainted or not.

I made sure to stay back far enough so he couldn't reach over and grab my gun. He didn't move or talk again. He didn't even rouse when Davis came stomping in the cabin with my canteen in one hand and some white cloths in the other.

"I found these pieces of cotton goods in the other cabin. They'll be enough to tie him up tight so he can make it down the mountain."

"Thanks, Davis."

I reached up to take the canteen in my left hand, and shook Blake awake with my right. He took three or four big swallows of the water and wanted more. I figured he better take it slow. I knew loss of blood caused a man to be thirsty, but I didn't want him to over do it. The water seemed to wake him up completely.

"What are you men doing here? I know you," he said, looking up at Davis. "I thought you burned up in the miner's cabin."

"You better wish I had, you skunk."

"You keep away from me." Blake pushed himself up a little more and sorta shrunk himself back tight against the bunk.

"This tall, skinny drink of water here and me are going to save your sorry life Blake, so shut up and don't aggravate us. You're not in any position to be doing that."

Blake dropped his head back against the side of the bunk. He looked as though he fainted, but I kinda had the idea he might be playing possum, so I kept on watching out for my gun while I helped Davis bandage him.

I held a thick, folded piece of the cloth front and back where the bullet had gone through Blake's side while Davis wrapped wide strips around his whole chest. We tied it off as tight as we could. He had an awful looking hole in his back where the bullet had come out, but it weren't no more than seeping a little blood.

We got Blake's wound bandaged, then picked him up. I took his feet while Davis carried his head. I think Blake really was out of it then. When we got down near the horses we put him down on the ground. Williamson came over to look down at him.

When he saw who it was he sort of grunted and asked. "Is he dead?"

"He's all right, I think." I answered. "He's lost a heck of a lot of blood from the looks of the floor up there, but we're going to try to get him down to Belden where there's a doctor to work on him."

"Well, blast it all anyway. I was hoping the sorry scudder was already in hell where he belongs."

Davis chuckled a little when Williamson said that. I pointed to the gray gelding. We untied the bags of gold that were on his back and tied some of them behind the saddle of each of the horses we were riding. We distributed what was left between the three animals that wore pack-saddles.

Both men helped me pick Blake up again and hoist him into the saddle. We tied his hands and feet and then tied him to the saddle. Davis and Williamson weren't any too gentle about it, but I figured that was understandable.

We climbed on our horses then and walked them back to the road that led down to Shell Lake and on to Belden. Even though we had redistributed the gold, the pack animals were still overloaded. I was leading the gray gelding that was carrying Blake. I sure hoped we would find the matching gelding peacefully grazing in that little patch of grass near my camp.

When we rounded the curve of the lake near camp I could see the glow of a fire. It looked to be right in front of my tent. I allowed it was probably Will Davis sitting by that fire, but I was ready. So were Davis and Williamson. We all had our rifles out, holding them across our laps. If claim jumpers had decided to try to move in on my property again, they were gonna be in serious trouble.

"Hello the fire." I yelled as we got close to the camp.

"Hello yourself," a woman's voice answered.

"Hetty Kendrick? What are you doing here?"

"Looking for you, you overgrown scalawag. What else?"

I got down and walked into the welcome glow of the campfire. Hetty came out of the tent still holding a double-barreled shotgun.

"Hey, it's only me."

"I can see it's you now but I couldn't know until you yelled."

"Well you don't need the gun now."

"Oh all right." Turning to the open tent flap she dropped the gun inside and came over to the campfire to give me a hug.

"Who are your friends? Oh, I see now. What in the world happened to you Evan Williamson?"

"Bless me, Miss Hetty, I been worked like a slave and half starved to death for weeks."

"Well everybody in town has given you up for dead."

"My wife and children too?"

"I saw Bessie yesterday, and she was packing up to go to her sister's. She's planning to leave town this coming Saturday evening as I understand it."

"I reckon she'll be downright disappointed."

"Now don't you say things like that, Evan. You know that's not true."

"I know that ma'am. My Bessie will be glad to see me still alive, for a fact."

"I don't believe I know you." Aunt Hetty said to Davis.

Sort of bowing since he didn't have a hat to tip, Davis answered "My name's Clement Davis, ma'am."

"You go on over to that yellow-topped wagon yonder, Clement Davis, and pound on the tailgate." Hetty said. "There's a boy in there that's going to be mighty happy when he sees you."

Davis grinned and said, "Thank you ma'am, I'll do that right now."

I put my arm around Aunt Hetty and we watched Davis walk over and hit on the tailgate of the wagon. Will's head popped out and he literally screamed when he saw his Pa's face looking up at him. He let himself fall right out of the wagon into his father's arms.

"Heck, I'm near-about crying."

"That's no reason for you to be ashamed of that, Wayne Kendrick" Aunt Hetty said, wiping her cheeks with her fingers.

"I ain't anxious for Williamson here to be telling all over Belden what a big baby I can be."

"Huh." Williamson said. "I hope there ain't nobody looking at me when I get back to my wife and kids."

"That reminds me. That Stinson fella I brought this mine from had a mule that looked a whole lot like that one right there."

"That is one of his mules."

"You mean to tell me those buzzards caught Stinson?"

"They did. They caught him, but he never worked in the mine. I saw him the day they brought him up to the mine. They had already put shackles on him and had him tied over the mule's back. When they threw him down to the ground he got himself up somehow and sort of shuffled and ran together down that track beside the aspens."

"That Gamble, one of the men that's dead up yonder, always carried a Greener. Blake motioned to him and just raised up his hand and pointed at Stinson. Gamble took a couple of steps to get in a better position and pulled the triggers on that shotgun. He fired both barrels at once."

"The shot tore Stinson's legs to pieces. Then Gamble and another guard took a hold of Stinson and dragged him out on that road that runs over to their hideout. It's the same one we come across. They dropped him in that deep arroyo that runs along the low side of it."

"My God, that's a awful thing to hear. Jim Cason told me a story about a man being shot and thrown down the side of the mountain while he was still alive. It's hard to believe men can be so lowdown.''

''That was a lowdown bunch of men, Kendrick. There's no getting around that. It seems to me like they got real satisfaction out of being as outright mean and vicious as they could manage to be.''

''When I bought this mine from him, Stinson mentioned to me that he had a sick wife and some kids waiting for him over to Colorado Springs. I'm going to ask Sheriff Dillard to count him out a share of this gold the same as you and the other men get. I'll take it over there and find his family. He was awful worried about them when he left my camp that day.''

''I'll go with you when you go over to Colorado Springs to find the man's family, Kendrick.'' Aunt Hetty said. ''It'll make it easier if I'm there when you tell that poor woman about her man.''

''I reckon you're right about that, Hetty, and I thank you. You sure will make it a lot easier for me.''

Clement Davis and Will came back to the campfire then. I was glad to see the smiles on their faces.

''Hey there Will. Did Jim Cason and that Blake girl make it down the mountain all right?''

''I'm sure they did, Ken. Cason was holding up real good. You'd have been surprised. The other gray gelding was here in camp when we got here, and they left here riding it double. I stayed to wait for you and then Miz Kendrick came up here a hour or two after.''

Hetty chimed in then. ''Jim and that girl came around by my house first, being that it was right on their way. They told me what was happening, so I decided to pack up some food and get up here to wait for you myself.''

''Jim said he was going to get Sheriff Dillard and go out to his father's ranch to get a bunch of men to ride with him up here to help you.'' Hetty said. ''They should be coming along any time now.''

''I hope Jim has sense enough to stay at home and rest that leg of his.''

''I wouldn't worry about that. The Major and Meg will make sure he takes care of himself.''

I walked over to the horses to check on Blake. It was a good thing he was tied in the saddle because he was still out.

Everybody crowded around the fire eating the food Aunt Hetty prepared for us, drinking coffee, and talking. About the time I was finishing up my second cup I began to think that maybe the Davis's would want to work this gold claim. I purely held no liking for mining, and I had plenty to do at home.

It wasn't even certain I'd be able to work inside that hole in the dirt. I wasn't worried none about the money I'd spent. I knew Jim would pay me back for anything I was out of pocket in buying the claim and setting myself up here.

''Say, that was more than delicious,'' I said. As I was getting up on my feet, everybody chimed in to thank Hetty for bringing the food.

''If you folks will excuse us, I need to talk some business with Will and his father, Hetty.'' I said, ''You and Williamson stay here by the fire. We'll walk on down beside the lake.''

Chapter Eleven

By the time Tom Dillard, Major Cason, and his men came riding into camp I'd made a deal for Clement Davis and Will to take over the mine. Will was going to ride with us to take Blake and the gold down to Belden. He would bank his Pa's share after he brought the supplies they would need to go on with.

We were just walking back up the hill from the lake when we heard a large group of horses running along the road toward the camp. As soon as they rode in, Major Cason swung down off his Morgan to walk over to me with his hand out.

"I can't thank you enough for sending my boy back to me, Kendrick." He said as he wrung my hand.

The major's obvious gratitude made me feel a little uncomfortable, but I knew he'd get over it soon enough. People like him didn't change. I decided to rub it in a little bit now while I had the chance.

Excusing myself for a minute, I walked over to the horse I'd ridden down to camp and pulled the big bundle of bank notes out of the saddlebags that Williamson had found in the outlaw's pockets. I walked back over to Cason and handed him the bundle.

"I sort of think this is yours, Major."

"My Lord, Kendrick. I can't believe you actually got my money back."

"Yep." I answered, watching his face as he struggled to find the right words. I finally began to feel a little ashamed of myself. I knew I had no business enjoying the man's discomfort so much.

"Forget about it Major. Evan Williamson found your money. He's the one you should be thanking and I know he could use some real appreciation. He lost everything he had when those crooks captured him.

"Evan was using his head and searched one of the outlaws we shot. I'd have walked off and left the money on the man's body. I was so anxious to get away from that place, it never even occurred to me to search those men."

"I'll go talk to Williamson," Cason nodded as he said. "I guess I owe him a reward."

I was tickled to know the Major appeared to have taken my hint, and hoped he'd be generous with Williamson. I turned to Tom Dillard, who was standing beside his horse. Ollie was with him, of course, but he was standing up close to the pack animals simply staring at those bags of gold.

"We need to talk about dividing this gold, Tom."

"Heck, Kendrick. We'll do whatever you want done, but don't it all really belong to Jim Cason?"

"He probably owns every grain of it according to law, Tom. But there's six miners down to Belden, and three others besides that are promised one thousand dollars worth of this gold apiece. They're entitled to that much and more, and I mean to see that they get it."

"I ain't going to quarrel with you none. You fix it how-some-ever you want it Kendrick. If they's any argument outta the Casons I'll just let you handle that too."

"That's a deal, Tom. Thanks."

Aunt Hetty stepped up beside me. "What are you men planning to do? Stay up here and talk all night?"

"Don't get in a big rush now, Hetty." I said.

"The Major is going to take his men up to the mine. They'll bring the bodies down. I'll ask Davis to be their guide. He can show them around the mine and then take them over to Blake's hideout to get the bodies.

"While they're doing that, Will's going with us to Belden to tend to his Pa's share of the gold. Tom here is going with us to town so we can put this crook in a cell and get a doctor to check on this hole in his side."

We watched as Clement Davis led Major Cason and his riders north around the lake. As soon as they were out of sight I helped Hetty get her things tied on the back of her horse and we started out toward Belden.

Hetty stopped off at her place. When I left there she made me promise to come get her when I got ready to ride to Colorado Springs to find Stinson's wife.

It was way too early in the morning for the town to be crowded. I was ready to bet most of those gold hungry strangers milling around the town the last time I was down here were long gone anyway. As soon as word got around that all the claims were gone from Shell Mountain there wouldn't be the least bit of need for those people to come to Belden.

We stopped at Tom Dillard's office and helped get Blake on a bunk in one of the cells. He looked bad, but he was probably too everlasting wicked to die. As soon as we locked Blake in a cell Ollie went to fetch Doc Holton. When I got ready to leave Tom followed me out of the office to stand on the boardwalk.

"Ken, come by here and get me when you head over to Colorado Springs. There's liable to be more of those skunks from Blake's gang hanging around over there."

"I don't think I'll have any trouble, Tom."

"Well, I heard Miss Hetty saying she was going with you when you go over there. It's a fair trip to Colorado

Springs, and you should have some help, just in case. I'd be proud to side you.''

It seemed like Tom was telling me more than he was saying. It came to me that he might be worried about Hetty going that far away. But it couldn't be that. *What the heck?* I thought. *It wouldn't make any difference if he rode to Colorado Springs with us. We'd be safer with an extra man along anyway.*

"I'll come by here and get you when I go to pick up Miss Hetty, Tom. It'll be a couple of days.''

With a big grin, Tom shook my hand. "I'm obliged, Ken. I'll be here at the office.''

Still thinking it was strange for Tom to be acting so concerned about me and Aunt Hetty, I untied my horse and motioned for Will to follow me to the bank. I noticed a group of men standing around in front of the saloon when we passed. I thought at first they were were strangers, but when we got close it turned out they were the six miners who walked down to town. The men looked so different clean and barbered and dressed in decent clothes I could hardly believe it.

Tom went and fetched banker Lane and it didn't take long for him to get the bank open. The miners came over and helped Williamson and me haul the bags of gold down off the pack animals and take them inside. We piled the bags up right in the middle of the floor. It was a sight.

Lane produced a scale and Williamson and me opened a couple of the bags to help weigh out about a thousand dollars worth of gold for each of the miners and Will Davis. I kept the poke we fixed up for Stinson's widow and promised the miners I'd go to Colorado Springs and find her before another week passed.

There was still enough gold to almost make banker Lane go to drooling. He was pacing up and down behind us the whole time we were working. I asked Williamson to stay at the bank and help Lane count the gold before he deposited it to Jim Cason's account. I don't really think Lane would cheat anybody, but I've always figured that even the best folks need somebody to help them stay honest now and again.

Will and me walked back out to the boardwalk with the group of miners. It didn't take long for us to say our good-byes. Those men were anxious to get their selves outfitted and go on home.

When Will left to go back up on the mountain I promised him I would ride up to the camp to see him and his Pa in a few days. I planned to do that the day I came back from Colorado Springs. But first I needed a chance to go home and rest and eat a few decent meals and make sure my life still existed.

I went to get Rollo from over to the livery, and refused to even answer Jake Ellis when he demanded to know where Hetty Hendrick's buckboard and horses had got to. He was making all kinds of noises when I rode out, yelling something about how he knew this was gonna happen.

Rollo was feeling good and tried to give me a hard time at first, but I just held on and ignored his shenanigans. I think I slept most of the way home. It was a good thing the horse knew the way.

Millie met me halfway to the barn. There was no doubt she was well over her mad, because she ran up and grabbed me in a big hug. I leaned down to kiss her and saw she had tears running down her face.

"I'm so glad to see you Kenny. I was scared to death. When you didn't come home I didn't know if something bad had happened to you or if you'd finally gotten so mad you left home."

"Now Sis, you shouldn't take on so. You know I'm always fine."

"I was in town when Jim Cason came in. I know what happened."

"Now, don't you take on about it. It won't half as bad as it sounds."

"You don't need to lie to me, Wayne Kendrick. I know better."

"I'm hungry."

"I figured you would be. Jim said he was sending a posse and you should be home today or tomorrow, so I cooked a big roast and a pot of vegetables. All I have to do is bake the bread. I can go ahead and do that while you clean yourself up. You and your clothes are smelling sort of ripe."

"Well, thanks a lot."

We walked over to the back porch and went inside. As we crossed the porch and entered the kitchen I was startled to see Jenny Drumheller sitting at the table holding a cup of coffee.

Turning to Millie, I whispered. "What's this?"

Millie's voice sounded a little bit stiff like. "Jim asked me to bring Miss Drumheller home with me. He feels he owes her a lot and he wasn't completely sure how his father would treat her."

Remembering my manners, I smiled and nodded to Jenny. "Good to see you again, ma'am. I reckon I owe you too, the same as Jim does. I know words ain't much but I sure do thank you for helping us."

I watched the young woman's face, trying to fit what Gamble had told me about her greed and cruelty into the picture made by her smiling face. I couldn't see anything but what I saw the first time I met her in the mine office. Her face and expression looked sweet and open and purely innocent.

"It's good to see you, Mr. Kendrick. I'm glad you made it out of that mess safely. We were worried sick about you."

"You shouldn't have worried about me. Jim knows I'm right particular careful to keep from getting myself hurt."

Jenny got up and went over to the safe to get another cup and poured out a cup of coffee. She sat it down on the table straight across from where she'd been sitting.

"Sit down Mr. Kendrick. I'm sure you need this coffee."

"I sure do need the coffee, miss, and I'm obliged. I'll not sit down yet, though. I'll take the cup with me while I go clean up."

It sure felt good to get myself clean and into clean clothes again. I'd had my boots on for so long it felt like they were trying to grow themselves onto my feet. When I finished dressing I slipped on a pair of slippers and walked back downstairs carrying my empty coffee cup.

"I smell biscuits." I said as I entered the kitchen.

"Come eat, Kenny. Everything's ready," Millie said.

Millie had set the table for all three of us. Besides the platter of hot biscuits there was a big roast, a bowl of steaming vegetables, and dishes of peach pickle. On the corner beside the biscuits there was a round of fresh butter and an open jar of Millie' own plum jelly. It looked like a feast to me.

I felt more than a little uncomfortable about Jenny Drumheller. I knew I probably owed her for saving mine and Jim's lives and that of several others. We might surely all be dead by now, except for her.

But I couldn't forget the way that Gamble talked about her. He hated her, there was no doubt about that. I kept slipping glances at her, trying to see signs of age in her face, but for all I could see she looked like the young woman she was claiming to be. I couldn't find any sign of the cruel nature that Gamble described.

After a while, when I got myself full enough to stop shoveling food in my face, I began to notice that Millie wasn't talking as much as she usually did. She hadn't looked over in Jenny's direction even once, either. The way her expression was it seemed to me like she was mad as fire about something or other.

I wondered if her mad had anything to do with the way Jim was looking at Jenny back up at the mine. Millie might have seen the same thing I did when Jim asked her to bring Jenny here to stay until he could take her to Denver and put her on a train.

"Tell me what happened at the mine after Jim and I left, Mr. Kendrick?" Jenny put her napkin back in it's ring and leaned forward to smile at me.

"There's not much to tell Miss. The miners got loose and we caught Blake and got back what gold he had."

"You didn't get that gold back without killing him."

It happened that I was looking right at her face when she said that. Something about her expression made me feel cold all over. It was just a flash I saw in her eyes. The change in her face was gone in an instant, but she suddenly stopped looking so young and innocent.

"As it happened, we did get the gold without killing Blake. He's wounded and right now he's locked in Sheriff Dillard's jail in Belden."

"I don't have to worry about him anymore then, they'll surely hang him."

"Jim explained that he promised to take you to Denver so you can catch a train to somewheres back east to live with your mother's sister?"

"I don't know what I'll do now that I know Blake's been captured. I was going to my aunt to get away from him. But I'll need to think about what I want to do now. Since Blake can't bother me any more I'm free to do whatever I want. I may decide not to go to my aunt."

Millie stared across the room at nothing. I would a sworn her face got even whiter—if that was possible. Whatever was wrong with her, I could see it had to do with this woman some way or another. The whole dad-burned thing was beginning to make me feel uncomfortable. I got up from the table and excused myself to go outside to smoke and think.

It sure felt good to sit on my own porch step in the quiet. Lights were on in the bunkhouse. Everything looked like it had ever since I was a kid. That was a pure comfort. I could hear dishes rattling as Millie and the Drumheller woman cleaned up from supper.

A man had to be thankful. That was one narrow escape. I'd been facing slavery for sure and the real possibility of a horrible death. I could easily have been chained in that cabin with the other miners when those guards set it on fire. It seemed to me then that nothing in this world could be better than sitting right there on my own back step.

The kitchen door opened and I heard footsteps cross the porch. As I stood up and turned around, I was surprised to see Jenny Drumheller through the screen. I was expecting Millie. I was certain she would come out and explain what had her so riled up before she went upstairs to bed.

As I stepped away from the door so Jenny could come outside, I looked up to see the lamp come on in Millie's room. I realized then that she must have been madder than I thought. *I don't think I've ever seen Sis mad enough to just clam up before.*

Jenny walked over to stand beside me.

"It's a beautiful evening, isn't it?"

"Yes, Ma'am."

"I'm sure you're glad to be home."

"Well, you've got that right."

"Let's sit here on the step and talk."

This was making me more and more uncomfortable. She was smiling and seemed to be crowding closer to me every minute. I went back over to the step and sat down on one end. The girl followed me and sat down right beside me.

Putting one hand on my arm she said, "I'm impressed by your ranch Mr. Kendrick. It's in a beautiful spot. From what your foreman says it covers several sections, clear over to the river."

"That's right."

I couldn't think of much to say. I guess I sounded sort of thick, and in fact I was feeling that way. It was pretty clear that the girl wanted to get a mite cozier than I was interested in doing.

"What's wrong, Kendrick?" She asked. Her voice was soft and she was smiling real pretty.

"Oh nothing. I'm right tired and I think I'll go turn in".

"I'm disappointed. I hoped we could talk a little while."

I stood up and sort of bowed. "Good night, miss."

"Good night fraidy-cat," She whispered.

It seemed to take forever for her to get up off that step and let me open the screen door to the porch. I almost ran in the back door, and through the house to go upstairs to my room.

Even with all the worry I had on me about Millie and that darn girl it didn't take long for me to go to sleep. I remember thinking *there's nothing like your own bed for a good rest*, and then I don't remember another thing. When I woke up it was right at morning. The hands would be in the saddle. I could hear Rich Thomas now. He'd be wise cracking with the men about me lying up here on my feather bed just burning daylight.

There was no sign of Millie when I got down to the kitchen, but there was a plate of biscuits and fried sausage in the warmer on top of the cook stove. I poured a cup of coffee, ate a quick breakfast, and took off for the corral.

Rich Thomas was standing in the open door of the barn talking to one of the hands. He raised his hand to wave and nodded when he saw I was headed for the ranch office.

It felt like I'd been gone away from the ranch for at least a month, though I had really only been gone a few days. Rich had taken hold and done everything just like I'd have wanted him to. I thanked him for that as soon as I could get a word in edgeways. He kept on and on telling me how glad he and the men were to see me home and in one piece.

He looked and sounded so relieved it sort of made me

wonder what Millie had done to the crew while I was gone. Rich and I spent the next couple of hours going over our plans for the roundup that was scheduled to start in less than a week.

When Rich finally left, I stood in the outside door of the office and smoked for a few minutes. About the time I finished my cigarette and started to head for the house I heard the sound of two horses coming up the lane. Jim and Meg Cason were coming around the corrals. My heart jumped. It was great to see Jim all cleaned up and mounted on one of his father's Morgans, but Meg was so beautiful in her blue riding outfit it hurt for me to look at her.

"Hello there," I said, taking off my hat.

"Hello Ken. I came to thank you for helping save my brother."

"Well heck fire Meg, you don't need to thank me. I just messed around until I got myself and another friend in trouble right along side of Jim. You need to thank Jenny Drumheller for getting us out of there."

"She'd never have gotten Jim free and back home if you hadn't gone up there to help him."

Meg got down off her horse and walked over close to me. That devilish Jim was standing there holding the reins of both the horses and grinning like a possum. He knew I was uncomfortable. It sort of irked me. He didn't have to look like he was enjoying it so dad-blamed much.

"Come on Sis," he said. "Don't keep embarrassing the man. Besides, I came over here to see Millie, not to stand here and watch you torture poor old Ken."

"You go find Millie and leave us alone you idiot." I said. I wasn't quite as uncomfortable as Jim seemed to want me to be.

"All right, for goodness sakes." He took off up toward the house. I didn't envy him dealing with Millie if she was still in the mood she was last night.

"Let's walk over to the arbor so we can sit down and

talk, Ken.'' Millie said, slipping one hand around my elbow.

My heart was thumping, and there was a kind of roaring in my ears. I felt a little bit like I did when I woke up after that outlaw pistol-whipped me.

When we got settled in the arbor, Meg was sitting fairly close to me. There wasn't enough room to do much else.

I sat there like a bump, and couldn't think of a thing to say.

Meg put her hand on my arm just like that Jenny had done the night before, but I sure reacted to it differently. Meg's hand was like a feather lying there.

She turned a little toward me and said, ''Seriously Ken. I am grateful for all you've done to save my brother.''

I held up my hand when she said that.

She hesitated a second, then kept on talking. ''Helped to save him then.''

''And on top of that Ken, you saved father's ransom money. I don't know how we can ever say thank you for all you've done.''

It was getting hard not to say something silly. I couldn't take my eyes off Meg's mouth. I'll swear she was looking up at me sweet and sort of inching her self over a little closer on the seat.

Finally, I couldn't handle it any longer. I bent my head and kissed her. It was just a little bit of a kiss, over in an instant. Her lips were soft. I watched her eyes open wide, then she sort of melted against me.

My arms wrapped themselves around her. She smelled like flowers. I held on to her for a minute or two, she felt so good. Finally I dropped my arms and eased back a little. Meg was looking up at me with a expectant look on her face.

For some reason the only thing I could think about right that minute was how upset Millie was.

''Do you know what's got Millie so upset?''

Meg looked sort of startled and pulled herself back over to her side of the bench.

"How am I supposed to know what's wrong with Millie? I haven't even seen her today." She sounded sort of put out for some reason.

"Oh. That's right. I was just feeling sort of concerned. She's been all white in the face and moody like ever since I got home yesterday."

Meg looked sort of disgusted and started to say something, but about that time Jim came stomping around the house looking like he could bite nails. He didn't even see us. He was headed for the corral.

I stood up and called out. "What's wrong with you Jim?"

He stopped and yelled back, "That sister of yours has lost her mind."

"Now what in the world do you suppose has happened?" I asked Meg.

"Let's go find out."

We walked over to where Jim had stopped.

"What is it Jim?" Meg asked.

"I went in the house to talk to Millie. When I went in the front Jenny was sitting in the parlor. I stepped in to speak to her. We chatted for a minute or two and about the time I went to ask where Millie was—I'll be doggoned if she didn't walk in the room right up to me and slap me across my face. Then she turned around and flounced out in the hall and up the stairs."

I was having a hard time to keep from laughing at first at the look on Jim's face. But this really was serious. I wasn't exactly sure what to say.

"Do you think maybe she found out that you and Jenny were a little too friendly while you were up there at the mine?"

"What the devil do you mean by a little too friendly? That girl took care of me when I was laid up with my leg broke and helped me get away from Blake. I owe her for that, and that's all."

"Okay, okay. Calm down."

"Millie acted like she hated me. She had promised to marry me when I left here last spring. Now she won't even talk to me."

"Do you think it's possible Jenny mighta got the wrong idea about something you said?"

"I said no."

"It's a sure thing something has got Millie riled up. She looked like death warmed over to me last night. I'll bet she hasn't slept for the last couple of nights. Maybe we ought to go talk to her."

"What are you thinking, Ken?" Meg interrupted to ask.

"I'm thinking maybe that Jenny girl said something to Millie."

"What could she have said to Millie to make her hit me?" Jim demanded.

It was kind of risky for me to say anything against Jenny to Jim. He hadn't heard what Gamble told Davis and me about her helping Blake, and being a lot older than she looked. He hadn't seen her eyes when I told her Blake wasn't dead either.

"Ken's right, Jim. You can't just stomp off. Let's go up to the house and talk to Millie." Meg said.

"Yeah, come on back with us boy, listen to your sister. Let's go straighten this thing out."

We walked in the back door together. As we entered the kitchen we heard the sound of angry voices from the front parlor. The words became clear as we hurried down the hall toward the room.

"I was upset before, but I don't really believe you. I can't believe you. Jim Cason would never do such a thing." Millie said.

"You might not know him as well as you think" Jenny answered. Her voice was a sneer. "Jim and I have been in love for weeks. Couldn't you tell that when he asked you to bring me home with you so I could get a chance to explain how we felt? He's probably too ashamed to tell you himself.''

''I think you're lying.''

Jim pushed past me and Meg and stormed into the parlor. He stopped beside Millie and yelled at Jenny.

''What are you saying to her, Jenny Drumheller? Have you gone crazy?''

Jenny's face just hardened. She looked exactly the way you would expect the kind of woman Gamble described to look.

''Never mind, Jim. I had to try.''

''What do you mean you had to try? I never said or did anything you could misunderstand. All I ever talked about were my plans to marry Millie and make a go of my ranch. How could you do this?''

''I don't want to talk about it.''

''Listen to me Jenny. I love Millie. We've been planning to get married for almost a year.''

Jenny's voice changed. Her words sounded as hard as she looked.

''It doesn't make any difference to me now, just forget it.''

Millie rushed out of the room and back up the stairs. I could see she was crying. Jim looked at Jenny for a minute, then took off up the steps after Millie.

I figured it was time for me to step in.

''I'd be obliged if you'd get your things together, Miss Drumheller. I think I'd better take you in to town. You can stay with my aunt Hetty until we can arrange for you to get to Denver.''

She stared at me for a moment, then turned away to go across the hall to the guestroom. She entered the room and slammed the door shut.

''Will you ride to town with me Meg?''

"Certainly I will, Ken. I don't blame you for wanting a chaperone when you have to ride around in a buggy with that woman."

After I stopped laughing I said, "It ain't that, honey. Considering what's going on with Jim and Millie, I think you and me have got some important things to talk about. I figure the ride back home from Belden will give us enough time alone to get our future straightened out."

Well, as it turned out, Meg and me sort of ignored Jenny on the way to Belden. I'm not all together sure how it happened, but by the time we got to Hetty's house Meg planned to go on to Colorado Springs with Hetty and me to find Stinson's family and dump Jenny Drumheller. Hetty agreed it was all right for Meg to go with us as long as she was there to chaperone. She only sort of raised her eyebrows as she showed Jenny to a guest room.

It took us the rest of the day to get the buckboard ready and go warn Tom Dillard to be at Hetty's house at daybreak the next day. Jenny stayed to herself and didn't say a word even when she sat in the back of the buckboard beside Hetty. She didn't help with getting supper or breakfast in camp or anything. Aside from Jenny being a pall, the trip was a joy with Meg sitting beside me all the way.

We got to Colorado Springs about the middle of the day. I noticed that morning that Jenny was dressed in Millie's second best traveling dress. I guess that sister of mine felt like she had to make up for feeling so hard toward Jenny some way.

Jenny tapped me on the shoulder and asked to be set down about half way along the street. I pulled over to the boardwalk so she wouldn't have to step in the muddy street. She didn't say a word. Just climbed down and grabbed her bundle. We watched as she turned around to disappear into the dressmaker's shop.

It was all sort of unsettling to me. I owed that girl my life, more than likely, and so did Jim Cason. But it was hard not to have bad feelings against her when I thought about the way she lied to Millie about Jim.

We asked around about Stinson's wife and children. We finally found out they had been staying at a rooming house out on the edge of town. Tom stopped off to talk to his lawman friend while we went out there. I gladly took Meg and Hetty with me to the door.

I had to knock twice before the door opened. The woman that finally opened up looked mean enough to bite somebody. I took off my hat and asked.

"Is Mrs. Hal Stinson in?"

"Who's asking?" The woman answered, straightening up and looking even more angry and resentful yet.

Wondering what the Sam Hill was wrong with the woman, I decided I'd better back up a little and let Hetty do the talking.

"We want to see Mrs. Stinson. Is she in?"

Hetty could freeze your ears with her voice, and she didn't hold back none. I could see she was plenty annoyed at the woman's unfriendly ways. She got her answer, but it was a shocker.

"Mrs. Stinson died last week. Doc said she had the pnumony. He done all he could, and so did I, but she won't strong."

I interrupted then. "Where's the children? Are they still here?"

The woman drew back some and began to look guilty.

"Those babies were too much for me. I turned them over to the town Marshall until he could find a family to take them. I couldn't be keeping them with no money to pay for their fixin's. I depend on renting my rooms to live."

Aunt Hetty got about a foot taller all of a sudden.

"Are you telling me you turned small children over to a man to be taken care of?"

"Get away from my door. I don't have to answer to you people."

"You wait just a minute." Hetty said. "Where are Mrs. Stinson's things? Did you give them to the sheriff too?"

Well that woman really commenced to look guilty then. It was amazing. I would never in this world have thought of such a thing.

"I kept her trunk and things to pay the last two weeks board. She had run out of money. It costs to feed a sick woman and two babies and I depend on my board money to live."

"You go get those things together this minute and bring them to the door. I'll pay you for two week's board."

Hetty's voice was steely, and her blue eyes showed how angry she was. The woman nodded and turned away, leaving the door standing slightly open.

"Go back and wait in the buckboard, you two. I'll wait for her to get the woman's things ready and find out where Mrs. Stinson is buried, then I'll call you to come and get the trunk."

I was plenty glad to get away from there, I'll tell you. We went over beside the buckboard to wait. I could see that Meg was as upset as I was. Those poor little young'uns. Lost their mother and father both, and turned out to be looked after by a lawman until they could be given away. I was about feeling sick again to think people could be so sorry.

It won't long before Hetty came sailing out of that house. She was still mad as a hornet.

"Go in there and get that trunk, Wayne Kendrick, and hurry up. This whole place stinks worse every minute."

Getting the trunk included getting another nasty stare from the woman. I figured Hetty went in the house to make sure the woman put most of Mrs. Stinson's things back in the trunk. Hetty must have paid her too, because she didn't say a word when I picked up the trunk, she just followed me to the front and slammed the door behind me.

When we got back to town, Meg and Hetty jumped out

of the buckboard before I could even help them down and marched into the town Marshall's office. I'll swear they looked downright scary to me.

Tom introduced us to his friend the Marshall. He was full of the story of how he had killed two of Blake's men in a shoot-out when what was left of the gang tried to rob the bank. Hetty listened for a minute or two, then interrupted them, demanding to know where the Stinson children were.

The Marshall never said a word. He just lifted his hand to point to the barred door of the cell at the back of the office. I went over to look in at the children. They were sitting together on the bunk. When they saw me looking in they both started howling at the top of their voices.

Hetty snatched the door open and entered. Meg was right behind her. Darned if those two little ones didn't stop crying and hold their arms up to be held. I reckon they saw how concerned Meg and Hetty were about them. I turned back to the Marshall to try to find out what was gonna to be done about those poor little things.

His answer wasn't very encouraging. "They're too little for me to get anybody to take the two together. I had one man ask, but I know for a fact he don't take much care of his own young'uns. All he wanted was to grow him some more hands to work on his rag-tag place. I told him he couldn't have these boys. Them there little'uns would be better off up to Denver in an orphanage."

Hetty and Meg came out of the cell, each holding one of the children. It was Meg that said. "These boys will not be going to any orphanage."

She turned to me then. I could see in her eyes what she wanted. I was about to say something silly, when I noticed the expression on Aunt Hetty's face. It was plain as day what I had to do if I didn't want my whole life turned up side down.

I turned to the Marshall as though I had been thinking

one thing all along. "We'll take the children, Marshall. This young lady and I are planning to be married right away, and we can take good care of them. Tom here can tell you, we're well off enough to see that they have a good home and respectable enough to treat them decent."

The Marshall agreed so quick you'd think Tom had already been talking to him about us taking those babies. Well we took them with us. I sat up in the front of the buckboard by myself all the way back to Belden. Meg sat in the back seat with Hetty and those two young'uns all the way. It was hard to think what those two could talk about so long, but I found out.

When we got back to Hetty's house they politely informed me that they had a double wedding all planned for the next Sunday right there in Hetty's house. I was to let Millie know and Meg would tell Jim. Also, we were to make sure to get there early for a dance the night before.